PRIMAL WARRIOR
DRACO AZUL:
SOULLESS BLOOD

Andres Perez and Ace Marrok

Edited by Lora Fitkin, Nick Fitkin, Matthew Dennion, Christofer Nigro, and Dustin Dreyling

Cover Artist: Elden Ardiente of Lungga Creatives

Table of Contents

PRIMAL WARRIOR
DRACO AZUL: SOULLESS BLOOD

PROLOGUE

In the outskirts of Chihuahua City, Mexico, various vehicles gathered around an abandoned factory as the town's seedy underbelly prepared for a night of moral decay. Criminals of differing ranks exited their cars, each with their posse in tow. From the factory stepped out the top enforcer of the man who organized this meeting. The tall, intimidating bodyguard inspected each and every visitor before allowing them entrance into the building.

Inside, the crime boss, Ángel, greeted his guests. He dressed in his most lavish attire as a means of flaunting both his wealth and power. His fingers were adorned with the shiniest of diamond rings. A leather suit jacket draped over a pristine white buttoned-up shirt. Lastly, his brown leather shoes looked like they had been bought that very day with nary a scuff on them.

Within the factory, dozens of delinquents hooted and hollered as they gathered around a wooden makeshift arena. Within the four thigh-high walls, two pit bulls ripped and tore at each other in a battle of life and death. Both canine warriors were covered in gashes and scars from numerous fights. Their mouths dripped with each other's spilled blood. The animals had been at it for almost two hours, the longest match of the night. One of the dogs' bodies was on the verge of collapsing as nearly every broken bone and torn muscle screamed in agony. Knowing his master would physically punish him if he did otherwise, the other canine stood his ground, defiantly. As tired as each canine was, neither wanted to give in to their opponent. Each combatant's only means of surviving the night was to become the last one standing.

The crowd grew more rambunctious as the end appeared in sight. No matter what was going to happen, one of these mutts wasn't coming out alive. These two beasts stared at one another. Neither flinched as they waited for the other to make their next move. The challenger was the first to step forward, but not before his femur gave way and snapped under its weight. With an opening in sight, the champion lunged at the crippled opponent.

With one final bite to the neck, the victor latched onto his enemy's throat and tore open his esophagus. Blood from the dying animal soaked the floor of the arena. The referee checked on the fallen canine and immediately declared the standing hound victorious. Many members of the audience cheered while others groaned at the loss of their underdog. Tens of thousands of pesos were waged in favor of the reigning champion, El Garras. The victor was soon taken by his owner, or his "Dogman," within the underworld of dog fights, while the loser was dragged away to be disposed of. Ángel set foot into the pit to announce the next match. His jewelry and flashy clothes glimmered in the spotlights.

"And there you have it, folks! El Garras stands tall once more!" the host spoke in Spanish. *"He only has one more match left before he becomes the grand champion! Who is crazy enough, dumb enough, and sick enough to try and take down this mighty beast?"*

Little did the audience know, El Garras was actually the host's dog all along, having been bred to be the most dangerous hound alive and given the best medical treatment money could buy. To avoid suspicion, the crime lord had virtually no contact with his prized pet. This way, he would be little more than a stranger to the brutalized fighter. The animal struggled to stay conscious because he knew that if he were to so much as lay down, he would be in for a severe lashing after the event.

El Garras's breathing slowed down, as did his heartbeat. He looked all around the warehouse to find people cheering in exhilaration. The dog did not know who these folks were, but it was the closest he felt to love any time he was forced to partake in the blood bath.

As antsy as the crowd was, not one single person wanted anything to do with the host's open challenge, especially after seeing the carnage that had just taken place before them. However, once the shouts and hollers died down, a lone figure slowly raised his hand. Not out of hesitation, but as a gesture of absolute confidence.

The middle-aged challenger was dressed rather inconspicuously. His hair was sloppy and dirty, his eyes were obscured in dark sunglasses, and his clothes lacked any sort of pizazz. In fact, they were slightly torn and covered in dirt. An unkempt beard adorned his face. From what anyone could tell, he was just some homeless guy. By his side was a male black Calupoh, a hybrid very foreign to dog fights where pit bulls have always been the standard. Everyone stared at the silent man and his wolfdog companion, utterly dumbfounded, before erupting into hysterical laughter.

"My God, you can't be serious," one man said.

"What sort of joke is this?" a woman asked.

"My mother's chihuahua has a better chance at El Garras than that scrawny, flea-ridden mutt!" Ángel uttered as he mocked the mysterious man and his jet-black hound.

This stranger never spoke a word, nor did his stone-faced expression change. He simply unchained his dog's collar and returned to his seat. The ebony canine walked into the arena, as if the beast knew where he was and where he needed to be. Once inside the ring, the Calupoh stood there, almost frozen in place. His eyes were still fixated on the host, never diverting his attention away.

The mysterious Dogman then raised his hand and uttered one single statement. *"This will all end in just five seconds."*

Ángel laughed off the challenger's preposterous claim. *"Heh heh, is that so? Very well then. Place your bets folks! Will El Garras reign supreme? Or will this absurd excuse for a fighter win tonight's tournament?"*

The audience cheered once more as new bets were placed. While the Calupoh's Dogman reverted to his unnaturally quiet self, making the surrounding gangsters anxious, his wolfdog continued to stand at attention as it waited for its opponent to enter. El Garras returned to the area, his wounds tended to and ready for another adversary to bite the dust. Once Ángel walked to his seat, having already welcomed all who were invited, he whispered into his lackey's ear.

"Who invited this idiot?" he demanded.

"I'm sorry, sir, none of us recall seeing him enter the warehouse. We thought he was a special guest."

"Well, he certainly isn't. Take care of him once El Garras tears his mutt to shreds. He's made a mockery of my tournament!"

Both dogs were inspected by the referee before the match could begin, making sure each canine was ready to fight to the death. Before the ref could even force the Calupoh's mouth open to inspect the teeth, the newcomer willingly displayed its jaws as if it were able to telegraph what the man was planning to do.

"Oh! I see you're well-trained. Too bad a dog like you is going to die very soon," the ref commented.

The referee then checked El Garras as the Calupoh waited patiently. The pit bull was determined to be able to fight, but upon setting his sights on his last opponent, he began to feel uneasy. He could sense a dangerous aura shrouding the mysteriously calm nature of the Calupoh. His small whimpers were ignored though as the referee yelled out to the audience.

"Let's go!"

The fight began as the audience roared for El Garras's victory. The pit bull snapped out of his fear-ridden daze and sprang into action. The mutt circled around the Calupoh, waiting for him to make the first move. Strangely enough, his opponent quietly sat in place, as if he was waiting on someone or something. The audience jeered at the dog to do something, but still he stood there, not flinching.

5

Ángel facepalmed in frustration before grabbing his lackey's tie. *"This is getting embarrassing. Get that mutt and his owner out of my sight. We'll deal with them later."*

Two henchmen stood up and headed over to where the Chalupoh's Dogman sat. All around him were attendees mocking both him and his pet. Before the musclemen could grab a hold of the dog's owner, the man latched on to each of their wrists and began shaking violently. El Garras, sensing danger once more, whimpered and leapt over the arena. Despite the other guards' attempts to capture him, El Garras's survival instincts kicked into overdrive and allowed him to duck and swerve around each and every thug before bolting out of the warehouse.

Before the gangster could get someone to reclaim his pet, everyone else's attention was drawn back to the Dogman. The sunglasses dropped from the stranger's face as he violently convulsed, revealing a pair of luminescent emerald eyes. Immediately, a bizarre green substance salivated from his mouth. He freakishly hissed at the thugs, before lunging at their throats.

The Dogman held each man's neck in his grasp, causing the two burly goons to gasp for breath. Then their bodies slowly twitched and convulsed as if they were suffering simultaneous seizures. It wasn't long before their skin and muscles took on an emaciated appearance. It appeared as if the Dogman was draining the pair of their blood.

Finished, the mysterious man threw the two lifeless husks to the floor. Each and every member of the crowd was horrified at the sight of the newly dehydrated corpses. What was especially disturbing were their faces, or rather, the lack thereof. Their duo's facial skin and muscles were ripped from their heads and still clutched in the claws of their attacker.

As the Dogman held both hands up to his face, he witnessed the remains of his victims absorbed into his body. Then his head slowly turned to face the host, a cruel smile

6

on his lips. At that moment, every unarmed member of the audience fled for their lives. Those that did carry firearms began unloading all of their lead on the savage figure. However, the Dogman twisted and turned his body in seemingly unnatural ways to avoid each and every projectile. He then dug his claws into the walls and climbed up to the ceiling before launching himself at the nearest group of gunmen.

The inhuman attacker did not perform the same excruciating torture of draining these gangsters of their blood, as he had done to his previous victims. In this instance, the man-beast chose to go directly for their throats with his claws and teeth like a tiger hunting its prey.

Meanwhile, Ángel sat petrified in his seat, too shocked to even comprehend what was transpiring before him. After killing and backstabbing numerous allies and foes along the way to the top of the criminal underworld, he figured he would no longer have to watch his back or constantly fear for his life. He thought he would spend the rest of his days in paradise, surrounded by pleasure and wealth. Yet it was at that very moment he realized that he was far from the top. The uninvited guest had not only made a mockery of his establishment but had also shattered the illusion that he was ever in any position of power at all.

Once all the men were slain, the Dogman stared into Ángel's terrified eyes. The beast-man began strolling towards the crime boss with a vacant glare and a snarling growl. As the stranger walked past his dog, still standing in the same spot, Ángel finally snapped to his senses and attempted to flee, running towards the backdoor exit. Angel felt a sharp surge of pain in his left ankle before his entire leg was pulled in the opposite direction of his salvation. He fell flat on his face and broke his nose.

The gangster wiped the blood from his nostrils and turned to see what had latched onto his leg. He saw nothing and turned his attention back to the door. Standing before him there was the Calupoh, which didn't growl or bark. Rather, it panted, almost as if it was excited about the slaughter. Dripping from the canine's mouth was blood, his blood.

"Get out of the way you mongrel!" Ángel shouted as he got ready to strike the dog.

Before he could, however, an immense force struck his back. It was the Dogman, digging his claws deeper and deeper into the man's back. He heard a loud snapping sound at the moment of impact. His body was then lifted off the ground and tossed aside like a rag doll.

Disoriented and coughing up blood, the gangster tried to get up, but something was wrong. He couldn't move his legs. In fact, he couldn't even feel his legs. Everything was numb below the waist, even from his ankle where the dog previously bit him. The man, who started the night in the lap of luxury, was now incapacitated, with his arms being his only means of locomotion left. He was no longer searching for an exit, as he only wanted to get away.

Angel could hear the Dogman laugh at his futile effort to get away. The laughs got louder and louder until the beast-man stepped on one of the host's legs, snapping it like a twig. Had the gangster been able to feel sensation from his now paralyzed lower extremities he would have screamed in agony. Instead, the man could only scream in fear at the realization of his own impending demise. Grabbing him by his shoulder, the stranger forced the man to look deep into his empty eyes.

"This will be over in five seconds," spoke the Dogman in a grimacing, almost inhuman voice.

In mere moments, the once untouchable gang leader was nothing more than prey, eviscerated on the spot.

The strange man dropped the corpse as he stared at his dog, still standing in place and panting. Suddenly, the ground shook beneath them, catching the pair off guard. Then the shaking intensified as the surrounding walls grew more unstable.

Was it an earthquake, thought the Dogman? No, it couldn't be, as tremors certainly weren't common in Chihuahua City. Just then, the inhuman being expressed a look of realization. He turned back at his dog. It barked, as if affirming the enigmatic being's thoughts. The pair slowly approached the front entrance. As soon as the two peered out from the factory's doors they witnessed a spectacular sight.

Two titanic beings of god-like stature fought for dominance in the middle of the city. One was a reddish-brown mammalian creature. However, this was no Earthly mammal, as it was not only gargantuan in size but also had two heads, one directly on top of the other. The other was an azure metal humanoid-shaped giant. This figure was equipped with blades on each of its forearms and a flowing red cloth hanging from its neck.

The Dogman remained unfazed by the spectacular battle taking place, while the Calupoh simply began panting once more.

CHAPTER 1

Buildings crumbled and the very ground itself shook furiously as the residents of Chihuahua City fled for their lives from the epicenter of the destruction. Within the heart of the town, various forms of rubble came crashing down, forcing men, women, and children to peer up at the sky with intense alertness. Towering above them was the cause of the ruination, two mammoth forms locked in mortal combat.

The two-headed creature with the stacked heads was unlike anything that had ever been seen on Earth, while the mechanical giant was easily recognized as the one and only Draco Azul. For nearly half a year, Mexico had been plagued by demonic behemoths whose only existence was to cause chaos, misery, and death. However, the beacon of light embodied by the azure knight was the only thing that staved off their invasion, swiftly slaying each monstrosity as it appeared.

Within the metal chassis of his super fighting robot, Eric Martinez struggled to subdue the beast before him. As the 26-year-old pilot moved his body, so too did the blue colossus, like that of a gargantuan mechanical puppet. Eric could feel whatever damage was inflicted upon his mech's armor, as well as see what Draco Azul's optical sensors detected, through an advanced suit and visor that he wore. Staring him in the face was the latest in a long line of the mysterious and ferocious beasts, the Diablos.

Eric fought to keep the beast's multiple jaws away from his robot's head (and torso). The abomination came ever closer at its face and began enveloping that of the metal titan. At that moment, the world slowed down as Eric weighed on the events that brought him to this very moment.

***

It all started on that horrific day months prior, when Mexico had been under constant attack by the very first of this hellspawn's brethren in Cancun. Several unearthly creatures all sprung forth from the depths of the Earth's crust within the ancient Maya city of Chichén Itzá. From there they spread out to the larger modern city, wreaking havoc upon its denizens and leaving the entire world gasping at their terrifying presence.

It was at that moment that Eric, on vacation from his home in Los Angeles, accidentally stumbled upon the very weapon he currently wielded. Draco Azul, a machine created long ago by benevolent extraterrestrials to face threats far beyond mankind's capabilities and was awakened in the present day to defend the planet once more. For the last 800 years, it was hidden away from the world. However, the moment Eric decided to use its power to aid the defenseless, he had drafted himself into a war that would push his mind, body, and spirit to the absolute limit. On that day he terminated the Diablos and hadn't stopped since, eliminating every such titanic beast that would dare rear its ugly face.

Today's encounter was with a double-headed fiend, covered in rust-colored feathers, a horned avian head sprouting from its chest, and another cranium above its shoulders that resembled a wild boar with large and sturdy tusks. Each of the Diablo's four limbs ended in three menacing talons. Its towering body possessed an elongated tail that tapered off into curled plumes. The beast's double craniums screeched in anger and lunged at their opponent, only to receive a strong metallic knee to the lower head.

With his enemy caught off guard, Eric followed it up with a roundhouse kick to the upper head. The force of the Primal Warrior's double combo forced the Diablo to the ground, crushing the smaller building underneath. As Eric caught his breath a voice was heard from his left.

11

"Watch it, kid! The whole place hasn't been evacuated yet. We gotta keep the fight from spreadin' out."

Beside Eric stood the holographic form of Ekchuah. The AI personality had been built by Draco Azul's alien creators to serve two major purposes. The first was to maintain the robot's multitude of functioning systems. Its second, and perhaps most important function, was to train those who were worthy enough to be pilots of the enigmatic mech. Ekchuah had the appearance of a Mesoamerican warrior. Standing at '6'5", the virtual muscular figure wore a large, feathered headdress, with jaguar's skin over his shoulders, and a loincloth. This visage was based on the mech's very first protégé from over a millennium ago in honor of both him and the Maya civilization that adopted the mech.

Harsh though his attitude was, deep down Ekchuah cared deeply about his pupil and only wished to prepare Eric for the life he signed up for. The AI had taught generations upon generations of pilots in the past, each with their own assorted stories to tell. Despite this, never before had Ekchuah encountered a student so underprepared for the battles ahead. Eric was neither a warrior nor a fighter. Throughout his life he avoided physical conflict at all costs. Yet it was the young man's decision to fight rather than flee that convinced Ekchuah to undertake his greatest challenge yet.

"I know, coach. But the thing was this close to pulverizing us!" Eric responded.

"Then pay closer attention. Do I have to keep reminding you? Look for any openings and don't lose your head!"

"Easy for you to say!"

As the two squabbled, a female voice intervened.

"He doesn't have to worry about losing his head. He just needs to deal with those two."

On Eric's opposite side sat a 27-year-old woman who had only recently joined his and Ekchuah's crusade against the Diablos, Ramona Escobar. Unlike the pilot, she wore contemporary clothing, which included a pair of jeans, a white short-sleeved t-shirt, and a black leather jacket.

A few weeks prior, her life as a bar owner changed the day Eric strolled into her hometown of San Cristóbal de las Casas. At the time Eric was lost, adrift in a sea of never-ending violence. Through their quick friendship, Eric found something he desperately needed, a connection to the outside world.

It was then that a Diablo had attacked the city, leading Eric to protect Ramona the only way he knew how, within the impenetrable armor of Draco Azul. Once the battle was over and her home and business were destroyed, Eric and Ekchuah offered to let Ramona tag along. To their surprise, the adventurous woman instantly agreed.

"You're right," Ekchuah acknowledged. "Those things certainly are quite a pain. We gotta take care of them first and foremost."

"Hmph, of course I'm right!" Ramona smirked.

"Hey, don't you go acting like Ekchuah, alright?" the pilot joked. "It's bad enough dealing with one of him."

"At this rate, you won't be dealing with either of us!" Ekchuah retorted, which was followed by a chuckle from Ramona.

With his head back in the game, the pilot witnessed the Diablo getting back up. The feathered abomination started dashing towards its opponent, claws stretched and maws gaping. Eric launched his mech forward in retaliation. The beast tried to swipe and slash at Draco Azul, but the great automaton dodged every blow thrown his way and countered using one of its fists.

Mounted on each of the mech's forearms was a massive, nearly indestructible blade that stretched over its hands. The resulting impact sliced through the face of the creature's chest-mounted head. Both entities screamed in agony as it clenched its injured cranium, bleeding through its hands.

"Attaboy, kid!" Ekchuah cheered on.

"¡Ándale, Eric!" Ramona followed.

Their celebration was cut short, however, as Draco Azul got a face full of intense heat blasted at its head. Through the technology in his skintight suit, Eric could feel an approximation of the intense damage the Diablo caused. His sweltering body, covered in sweat, was pushed to the point of exhaustion.

"Agghhh!"

"Eric!" shouted Ramona.

"You alright, kid?" asked an alarmed Ekchuah.

"I-I'm okay."

Eric tried to peer out from his blurred vision, where he saw two shining lights coming from a mahogany-colored blob.

"Heads up," Ekchuah warned. "That thing's gonna fire two shots this time!"

The Diablo unleashed twin beams of pure, concentrated plasma energy at its azure foe from each mouth. With no time to respond, Eric raised his arms, ready to embrace the brunt of the impact. At that moment, his arms and chest suffered an incredible amount of anguish as the plasma projectiles proved to be more than he could handle. Despite Eric's best attempts to stand his ground, Draco Azul was knocked off its feet and crashed into the streets below.

As soon as the young man regained consciousness his attention quickly shifted toward his teammate. He switched views from his robot's to his own.

"Ramona! Are you alright!?"

"I'm fine," the young lady answered, still strapped to her seat and clenching onto her skull from a headache brought on by the whiplash.

Surrounding her were blaring sirens and red lights flashing inside the cockpit.

"What's the damage?" the hologram asked her.

She quickly scanned through the holographic screens placed before her, each depicting various statistics. "Well, you can forget using the Draco Striker. We don't have enough energy for that."

"Damn!" Eric shouted.

As powerful as his mech was, it only had so much power before it needed to be recharged. With every battle, he and his team endured, more precious fuel was depleted. The robot's only means of recharging was to absorb lightning, and unfortunately for them, there was not a storm in sight for miles.

"Looks like we're gonna have to do this the old-fashioned way," Ekchuah suggested to his protégé as he got back up.

Finding another opportunity, the Diablo discharged another plasma attack, only this time Eric saw it coming. Draco Azul sidestepped at the nick of time as the lasers hit one of the many mountains surrounding the city. At that very moment, Eric knew he had to go in for the kill and bring an end to their duel. With determination, the young fighter shouted a single phrase.

"Draco Fangs!"

As soon as the voice recognition software activated, the two blades that adorned his robot's forearms ejected from their positions, revealing a grip along each tool. Through Eric's quick reflexes, Draco Azul seized its new handheld weaponry before they could even hit the ground below. With his blades now in hand, the metal goliath ran towards the Diablo.

The monster tried to take the mech down with yet another set of plasma beams, and this dual of projectiles rapidly approached their target. Not being able to dodge in time, Eric had his sapphire-hued metal avatar hold up both blades in front of itself like a makeshift shield. Miraculously, the beams bounced off the sabers.

Draco Azul then ducked down and aimed its right sword at the Diablo, slicing off its right leg from the knee down. The beast wailed as it lost its footing, both figuratively and literally, and its top head stared up at its combatant as the robot stood over it. The last thing it saw was another blade swiping at its face before its vision went completely blank.

"Nice thinking, kid," Ekchuah complimented.

"How did you know that would work?" Ramona asked.

"Heh, I didn't!"

This revelation shocked his female companion.

"Are you crazy? You could've killed us!"

"Hey, sometimes a warrior's gotta improvise and hope for the best," defended the AI mentor. "I'm just glad you started relying more on Draco's tactical advantages."

"Yeah, I can't always rely on brute for- *woah*!"

Before Eric could finish his thoughts, he felt a sudden sharp pain in his left leg before he was pulled down by his still-living foe.

Having the top portion of the boar head's skull chopped off, the remaining cranium took control of its mutilated body, directing the creature to crawl over the metal guardian's frame and claw at its chest. Draco Azul attempted to lift its arms but was quickly pinned down by the Diablo's own limbs. The monster leered at its foe and opened its jaws in preparation for one final plasma assault. Suddenly, the elongated scarf that once draped over the metal goliath's back sprang into action. The crimson garment wrapped itself around the demon's left arm and pulled it away from the mech.

With his right hand free, Eric thrusted the metallic knight's saber directly into his enemy's face. Its body twitched violently and the red glow inside the creature's jaws quickly faded. In a few short moments, the creature's entire body went limp before falling on the mech. Soaked in its enemy's blood, Draco Azul shoved aside the beast's corpse and stood tall once more.

Eric scanned the entire area to assess the destruction that wrought Chihuahua City. All around him he saw buildings destroyed, streets decimated, and most mournfully, corpses. While the young man grimaced at the thought of the numerous people he failed to save he also took notice of the growing crowd of survivors. The exhausted citizens were slowly crawling out of their shelters now that the carnage was over. He may not have been able to rescue everyone, but he was at the very least able to prevent a significantly further loss of life.

This sentiment was also shared between his teammates. Ramona grabbed a hold of her gold rosary and performed the sign of the cross. She silently prayed that the spirits of those lost in the battle may find peace in the afterlife, and that their loved ones find strength in God and each other.

Meanwhile, Ekchuah looked over the two of them, worried how his companions were taking the grave news. He warmly smiled as he witnessed each of his friends accepting their simultaneous victory and defeat. It was never an easy job to take on the mantle of a protector, let alone the teacher of one. Though he could rest easy knowing that together the three of them can, and will, get the job done.

An exhausted Eric sighed freely now that he could finally relax. He removed his visor as he turned to see his teammates with his own eyes.

"How was that, guys?"

"Eh, six out of ten," Ekchuah remarked.

"Yeah, could've been better," an equally unimpressed Ramona added.

"What? Come on, it wasn't *that* bad."

"Well, you did leave yourself open a few too many times there," said Ekchuah.

"Plus, you didn't even use your scarf until the very end," Ramona followed.

"Whose side are you guys on here?"

"The side that doesn't want to see you get your ass kicked," Ramona answered.

Eric sighed in utter defeat while his friends laughed at his misery. However, he could not help but admit that they were right. For as much as he'd improved as a fighter, he still had much to learn, especially if he planned on protecting everyone.

"By the way, kid," Ekchuah commented, "you might want to take a look at the screen."

A holographic display appeared before the three of them. The floating monitor presented the real-time recordings of Draco Azul's many cameras. There, the trio witnessed hundreds of townsfolk that had come out of hiding to cheer on their victorious champion. Eric then placed his visor back on so that he may get a personal look at the public through Draco's own eyes. On the ground level, the men, women, and children who surrounded the two-hundred-foot-tall robot could see the mech stare down and give everyone a thumbs up, the ultimate sign of positivity.

Dozens applauded the acknowledgment and many more took various photos of the occasion. With their job done, Ekchuah called out to his pupil.

"Alright, kid. That's enough indulgence for now. Let's head out."

"Heh. Alright, coach," a smiling Eric responded. He then gazed up at the starry night sky and shouted one more phrase. "Draco Wings!"

Two large, jet-like fins extended out of Draco Azul's back, which then ignited and propelled the metal goliath into the sky.

CHAPTER 2

Over the course of the following day, the remains of the Diablo were heavily quarantined by both law enforcement and military personnel. This was the standard operating procedure for every gigantic creature that terrorized Mexico, at least those that the equally mysterious robot hadn't already obliterated. Surrounding the beast was a hastily built fence comprised of towering metal panels, blocking the deceased monster from prying eyes. Only one entrance was set up in front of the creature's top cranium. As an extra layer of protection, a chain fence was placed on the outer perimeter of the area. Contained within were various trucks, tanks, tents, and labs set up all around the monster.

Guarding the titanic cadaver was Sgt. Lucas Garcí and the fifty soldiers under his command. All were positioned around the deceased creature's body across a 500-meter periphery. When he arrived at the base hours prior, he was petrified at the size of the behemoth, having never seen one up close before. The soldier had to use every ounce of mental fortitude to keep himself from going insane within the vicinity of the otherworldly being.

The actual smell of the decaying carcass didn't help matters either as the putrid odor was enough to make an entire butcher shop's worth of rancid meat seem like a flower garden. He had to spend all day keeping his men in check so as not to lose their minds. For Lucas, this was the first time he and his platoon were ever assigned the crucial task of protecting a Diablo base, an unenviable task for many.

As with all of Draco Azul's fallen foes, a military camp had been set up around its remains within twenty-four hours, complete with the presence of the Mexican armed forces. With each new corpse, more and more troops were deployed as the threat of illegal profiteers grew steadily. Often, it was gangs and merchants that attempted to steal and sell samples of blood, flesh, and bone on the black market. Individuals, organizations, and even entire corporations, both in and out of Mexico, paid top dollar for the chance to procure the most valuable biological material in the entire world. Some sought to secure a sample for the sake of owning such an item, while others wished to reverse engineer the raw genetics for medical and military uses.

As domestic and international interest in the Diablos grew, so too did the strength of the Mexican government's forces. If unprepared, they would usher in a new age of biological warfare. As much as they wanted to utilize the monsters' own biology against them, their ongoing invasion had left the country far too crippled to afford the resources necessary for such a herculean task. Until the time came for Mexico to recover and flourish, the government had to reluctantly rely on the elusive and wondrous mech the public had dubbed "Draco Azul" for the time being.

As the hours rolled by, Lucas periodically checked on the scientists behind the barrier that separated them and the Diablo from the rest of Chihuahua City. All throughout the night, they stood in their tent by the beast's second cranium, performing test after test in an attempt to comprehend its surreal physiology.

For the past several months, Mexico's top minds studied and analyzed each deceased specimen. Beyond their violent and destructive natures, no two subjects shared any similarities within their genetic structure. What left biologists especially baffled was that despite seemingly appearing from deep within the Earth's crust, the creatures' genetic information did not resemble any of Earth's known creatures in the slightest. Even more puzzling was why only one of each supposed "species" of Diablo had appeared so far.

Unfortunately for the human race, Eric and his friends had also remained mystified by the cryptic origins of these various abominations. Although the pilot and his AI mentor were almost certain these creatures were not from their world. However, such a thought raised even more questions and graver thoughts.

"Hey, sarge," Lucas's lower-ranking squad mate and friend, Sebastian, called in a clearly nervous tone.

"Yes, private," he responded, trying to cover the mutual anxiety he too was experiencing.

"You ever wonder, you know, about these things?" Sebastian nodded towards the gigantic corpse.

"What do you mean?"

"Well, are they a sign from God? Or even the Devil?"

Sebastian was always the most religious of his team, and it was clear to Lucas that he had taken the moniker of "Diablo" quite literally.

"That's what we're trying to find out. Until then, they're just big animals and nothing more, Private."

"You know what I think? It's a sign of the end of days. The Apocalypse. Pretty soon, I bet there'll be an entire army of these things ready to take on the world!" The breathing in Sebastian's voice grew heavy as he divulged his beliefs.

Lucas had to think of something to calm his men down. Otherwise, he'd be responsible for letting a massive panic get out of hand. He was well aware that fear can be incredibly infectious in stressful times.

"Well," he responded. *"What does that make Draco Azul?"*

"Huh?"

"If the Diablos represent this so-called 'end of days,' then why is the big guy trying to stop it? God couldn't be trying to wipe us out if he'd also sent a protector."

Lucas wasn't so keen with relying on such a dangerous wild card, especially one as equally unfathomable as the metal giant. Yet, as suspicious as he was of the mysterious entity, he knew it was the only thing keeping Mexico from devolving into chaos. As long as the threat of the Diablos existed, he was going to have to put his faith in the titanic warrior.

"Say, you're right. It could be that God hasn't forsaken us and that the Diablos are the minions of Hell, rebelling against all creations of the Lord." Sebastian's breathing subsided noticeably.

"Sure, that very well could be. But in the meantime, we gotta prove our worthiness to God. Got that, soldier?"

"Yes, sir!"

***

An hour passed and still no sign of anything unusual had been detected by Lucas and his squad. Once he confirmed that the scientists were safe, the military man went back to surveying his section of Chihuahua City with two of his subordinates. That's when he heard a soft flapping noise up above. The sound was immediately followed by a light gust of wind that blew down the soldier's back. It was as if someone was moving a tarp or blanket up and down with extreme force. He peered up, only to find nothing. Lucas looked to his comrades.

"Did any of you feel that?" he asked.

He found that they too heard and felt the exact same thing. All three readied their rifles and radioed his men.

"Everyone, we may have an intruder in the vicinity. Stay alert for any potential threat."

As much as the guard physically and mentally prepared himself for the presence of any looters, Lucas could see nothing but the various buildings that had remained vacant since the evacuation was ordered. *Perhaps it was just a very large bird,* the army man thought.

Moments before he could relax however, a wet substance landed on his left shoulder. He looked down at what appeared to be a slimy green substance running down his arm. The soldier touched the ooze with his hand. A slight burning sensation was felt as soon as his skin made contact.

A loud hiss got the attention of all three men, and soon additional bursts of wind rained down on them.

"Above us! Open fire, men!"

Fear ensnared Lucas and his brothers-in-arms as they unleashed a barrage of bullets into the air. The sergeant quickly regained his senses and told his men to cease fire. Raining over their heads was a wet material. It didn't have the same texture as the ooze from before. This substance was thinner, almost like blood.

Suddenly, something massive hit the ground with a loud thud just meters away from them. Lucas ordered his men to flash their lights at the object, which was revealed to be a bizarre, almost human-like being. The creature groaned as it lifted one of its elongated arms. Between each extended digit was a torn, thin layer of skin. Whatever this thing was, it was unlike anything they had ever seen.

Other soldiers nearby radioed in asking what the commotion was. As his men responded, a strange sight caught his eye. Directly in front of them, standing perfectly balanced on the fence that separated them from the rest of the city, stood three pale-looking men. Each one of them was shirtless and barefoot with ripped pants. Their bodies were adorned with multiple bullet wounds. The more Lucas observed these intruders, the less human they appeared. What caught his eyes the most were their sharp talon-like nails, black eyes, green pupils, and green ooze salivating from their mouths. It was the very same gunk that stained the soldier's sleeve.

Lucas was extremely baffled. He tried wrapping his mind around what was happening. How were they effortlessly balancing on the fence? How did they manage to sneak past him? Most perplexing was how they caused all those sounds moments prior in the air. The soldiers all aimed their weapons at the trio.

"You three are violating restricted space," Lucas decreed. *"Surrender, or we will be forced to use lethal force!"*

All they got in response was the deathly gaze of the ghoulish beings. As Lucas was about to radio in, one of the figures leapt off the fence and into the air with inhuman strength. The intruder landed on top of Sebastian before he even had a chance to fire his rifle. The force of the landing was enough to break the soldier's ribs. Lucas could hear the man's bones snap over his screams of agony.

The second ghoul leapt onto the third in command. He managed to send several bullets in the monstrosity's direction, stopping the creature dead in its tracks. Before he could help his downed ally, two more of the pale beings ambushed him from the darkness. With both men pinned to the ground, the inhuman creatures thrust their claws into their victims and ripped them apart like hunters digging into their prey. Lucas immediately called in for backup as he began firing on the increasing intruders.

"Everyone, we're under attack!"

Rather than a confirmation, the only responses Lucas received were more screams from both his radio and even in the distance. It appeared that all of his men were under attack and were overpowered by the sheer number of their strange foes. His thoughts went towards the scientists, who were his top priority. They were under his protection, and he was willing to lay his life on the line if it meant preventing these things from laying a finger on them.

Just then, one of the original three ghouls jumped in front of him. Strangely, this one did not attack him. In fact, none of them were. They all simply stared at the lone man. Lucas had no time to question their actions, for he needed to get to the scientists before they did. He ran past the motionless intruders, but not before leaving an unpinned grenade next to the nearest enemy.

Closer and closer he ran towards the gate, summoning every ounce of strength he had to escape the explosive's range. That's when he heard the grenade go off. He didn't look back; rather, he punched in the password on the keypad and entered the camp.

"What's going on?" shouted one of the panicked biologists.

"We're under attack. Everyone else may already be dead," Lucas bluntly responded as he grabbed whatever tables and chairs he could gather to barricade the closed gate. *"We're dealing with something that ain't human."*

"Something not human?" questioned a stupefied zoologist.

"You heard me. Those things look human, but they tore my men apart like they were nothing but cardboard. Call for reinforcements while I take care of this!"

Once the message was sent, Lucas had his sights set on the entrance. That's when he had a sudden realization – these things were above him prior to their attack. This meant they had the ability to fly. Not just that, but they could easily hop over the fence. Still, none of them were making any attempt to force their way in. All he could hear were the sounds of more individuals gathering around the gate.

That's when the sound of screeching metal could be heard on the opposite side of the ferrous wall. Lucas readied his rifle while the five individual scientists panicked behind him. The commander grabbed his pistol and handed it over to the one shaking the least.

"As soon as they clear the entrance, I want you to lay into them!"

The man was too scared to resist and quickly aimed at the door. With superhuman strength, a lone figure tore open the metal gate that surrounded the massive carcass. However, this creature didn't resemble the ghouls in the slightest. It was a man dressed in a plain business suit and sunglasses. His hands, though, were equipped with razor-sharp nails that had previously cut through the ten inches of reinforced steel. Huddled around him were more ghouls. Lucas figured this had to be their leader.

"Fire!"

Despite being shot at point-blank range, several of the ghouls jumped away. Each one was hit with round after round of Lucas's and the scientist's assault rifles. While a few stray projectiles tore through his clothes, the figure managed to survive the barrage of bullets with not a single scratch on his person. Lying on the floor were the five followers that weren't so lucky.

The intruder grimaced as he stared at his fallen comrades, then proceeded to walk towards the two armed men. He grabbed Lucas by the neck and tossed him against a wall like a discarded doll. The sergeant felt every bone in his body shatter upon impact. Drifting in and out, he struggled to remain conscious, fighting every urge to succumb to his injuries. All he could witness was the intruder seemingly interrogating the scientist.

"You will tell me what you have discovered as to the nature of these... 'Diablos,' or else you will die a painful death."

"O- ... A- ... K- ..." Were the only sounds that escaped the scientist's mouth. As much as he tried, he was far too petrified with fear to utter even a single coherent word.

Annoyed, the intruder raised his other hand. With a snap of his fingers, a ghoul rushed inside and attacked one of the ten remaining scientists whose backs were against the gigantic corpse. Within seconds the grotesque creature had devoured its victim's heart.

"Do I make myself clear?" the intruder spoke, this time in a stern tone reminiscent of the way a parent talked down to a child.

"Y-y-yes!" the scientist shrieked now that he had managed to scramble together his senses.

"The Diablos aren't related to any known species on Earth."

"Anyone can figure that out!" shouted the intruder, whose patience was quickly running out.

"I want to know if their blood contains the same nutrients and oxygen as those of humans and animals?"

Their blood? thought Lucas. *Why the hell would he want to know about that?* Just then, it struck him. The ghouls all preyed on his squads, like vampires in a horror film. Was it possible that they were planning on feeding on the Diablo?

"Y-yes," the scientist whimpered. *"W-we discovered last month that their blood delivers the same substances to and from their cells. The ratio of plasma, water, and red blood cells varies among specimens, but they all function the same. Their blood is fundamentally identical to all known animals."*

"Humans included?" the interrogator spoke as he squeezed his victim's neck.

"Ack- Yes! Yes!"

"Thank you for your time."

The devilish grin returned as he spun around and threw his subject to the crowd of ghouls behind him. Each of them tore into the poor man like piranhas.

A shot rang out and a bullet struck the intruder's head. But rather than falling, he simply dug into his skull and extracted the piece of metal that had embedded itself into his cranium. He turned to see Lucas, on the ground a few feet from where he had previously laid. In his hands was a now empty revolver, having fired its last remaining shot.

"How precious."

It was then that a Calupoh entered the lab and stood next to the man. Before turning to the intruder, it looked up at the massive mound of rotting Diablo flesh. The pair stared at each other for some time before the man turned towards his mob of monsters and raised his clawed hands.

"My brothers and sisters," the stranger preached. *"For too long have we been forced into the shadows. Too long has humanity halted our evolution. Denied us of our prosperity!"*

The man thrust his claws into the chest of another researcher, killing her instantly and tossing her aside. He then sunk both hands into the flesh of the giant monster, its blood pouring out like a crimson fountain. Cupping his hands, he proceeded to drink the viscous fluid. Now bathed in the scarlet ichor, he turned to his audience.

"Now, drink this life-giving nectar and transcend beyond your wildest dreams!"

As if on command, the ghouls scurried to the flowing blood and began to feast on not just the Diablo, but the remaining scientists. Lucas was helpless to save any of them as he had used the last of his strength to get his broken body to the closest weapon he could find. Before long, he noticed several of the ghouls heading towards them. Each of their mouths dripped fresh Diablo blood and saliva that illuminated a chilling glow.

He knew then and there that his time was up. All he could do was pray that wherever Draco Azul was, it would carry the torch and succeed where he had failed. He never thought he would have put his faith in a being he distrusted so much. However, if the mech was indeed the savior his friend Sebastian believed in, then he was left with no choice but to place all his faith in the metal giant. As the ghouls huddled around him, he heard the blood-drenched stranger utter one final statement.

"Indeed, we shall cleanse this world of man, for the age of the Naguals is upon us!"

CHAPTER 3

Fists flew against the backdrop of the rising sun as Eric and Ramona engaged in their daily morning training session. Behind the pair was the towering form of their giant robot, casting convenient shade from the summer heat over them. This sparring match was the latest to take place between the rookie pilot and the former bar owner. Having a father who had taught her how to survive the harsh streets of Mexico, Ramona was more than capable of going toe to toe with the pilot of the Primal Warrior. At her suggestion a week ago, she offered to be the perfect candidate to act as his sparring partner.

Prior to their one-on-one face-offs, Eric had solely been trained by Ekchuah, who instructed him in the many uses of Draco Azul's attributes and abilities. On top of that, the holographic coach had to teach the young man everything he knew about fighting from both his programming and his past pilots. His form of martial arts was one based on reactive maneuvers designed for self-defense, paired with swift and deadly strikes for finishing off dangerous opponents. At the very start, all of Eric's drills took place within the cockpit as he brawled with Ekchuah directly while the pilot suit allowed the AI to make physical contact with its wearer. Yet, for as skilled as Ekchuah was in combat, going toe-to-toe with Ramona was an entirely different experience.

For every punch lodged at the dexterous woman, she dodged with grace. Ramona's light weight gave her speed and agility that was far greater than his coach. For every move she avoided, the young lady countered with a strike of her own, normally in the form of kicks. Never before had Eric struggled to keep up with such a swift opponent. Prior to meeting her, his rogue's gallery consisted of large, lumbering titans, or the powerhouse that was Ekchuah. Besides her swiftness, the other major difference between the AI and the woman was that she was a flesh and blood person. Every impact she landed was far more real than anything his pilot suit could simulate.

Ekchuah may have put Eric through hell, but there was something about his trials with Ramona that gave him greater clarity. It gave the hero-in-training the chance to stay on his toes and enhance his reflexes, not to mention pulling his punches so as not to exert too much strength and tire himself out so quickly.

Above the two fighters, Ekchuah oversaw his pupil's conditioning from within the metal chassis of Draco Azul. The giant mech sat flat on the ground with its eyes aimed at the pair. Surrounding the machine was a vast array of mountains and cliffs. It was perfect for obscuring the large figure located inside the Copper Canyon situated within the larger state of Chihuahua. As the hologram supervised his student's morning regimen, he was simultaneously browsing online for the latest news regarding Diablo attacks.

Eric leaped into the air to deliver a mighty kick at his opponent, followed by several punches. However, she had the foresight to see this move coming and dodged the kick before successfully blocking the next two attacks. Throughout her childhood, Ramona had witnessed many free-for-alls. These brawls typically involved her biker father, a local hero where they grew up. Any time a troublesome punk or dangerous criminal disrupted the peace, he made sure to settle things, even if it meant using sheer brute force.

Despite his vigilante lifestyle, he made sure to keep his only daughter away from any and all physical altercations but nevertheless bestowed upon her the knowledge to protect herself should the need arise. After his life was tragically cut short, the vigilante's daughter was left to fend for herself, something she was equipped to handle in the rough and tumble world she lived in. When fate guided the young woman into becoming the third member of Team Draco, she decided to wear her father's leather jacket into battle so that she may carry on his fight for justice.

Seeing an opportunity, Eric prepared a push kick aimed towards his sparring partner's stomach. Barely catching her opponent at the right moment, Ramona grabbed his foot with her free arm and flung him to the dirt. The biker's offspring quickly pounced on Eric's chest, ready to strike.

The young lady flung her fist at his face but halted right before it hit. Eric looked up to see a grinning Ramona.

"Good match, but you still got a lot to learn." Her fist opened to reveal a helping hand to Eric, who smirked back as he took it. "You're definitely improving, but you're leaving yourself open to your opponents. Especially around the legs."

"Hmph. You're not the first one to say that," the youthful warrior begrudgingly admitted.

Eric was irritated at being reminded of his shortcomings in combat. Unlike Ramona, he was never a fighter prior to becoming Draco Azul's pilot. Throughout his life, fighting was the last thing on his mind. Any time he found himself in a confrontation, be they physical or verbal, his immediate response was to run. Yet, on that fateful day, when he had stumbled upon that towering automaton, something within him changed. A new side to him emerged, the sense to fight rather than fly.

Years of anguish and rage caused Eric to reach his boiling point, giving the mech pilot the fuel he needed to stand his ground. However, this new instinct was still in its infancy. If Eric was to harness his newfound courage, he needed far more time to train his mind, body, and spirit. Unfortunately for him, time was a luxury he did not have. In other words, the more assistance he had in honing his skills, the better.

"Any more dirt you wanna throw at me?" Eric jokingly asked Ramona.

31

"Avoid relying on your beams and scarf. Your fists and feet can be just as effective," Ramona suggested.

"No sweat. With your help, it'll be a cinch!"

"We'll see- wait, what?" Ramona asked.

"What do you mean 'what?'"

"That thing you said. 'It'll be a cinch.'"

"Yeah?" Eric asked before realizing what his friend was confused over. "Oh! It means 'it'll be easy.' Y'know, nothing to worry about."

"Like, 'piece of cake?'"

"That's it!" he confirmed.

"I see," pondered Ramona. "I've heard of that one, but not 'cinch.' What does it even mean?"

"I-I don't know. It's something we always say in America." Eric paused for a couple of seconds before he realized what he and most likely numerous other Americans would've thought. "Come to think of it, I'm pretty sure most of us don't know where it even comes from."

"I swear, English doesn't make any sense," Ramona chuckled to herself. "But thanks. I still struggle with English slang. Back home, I would sometimes get confused over what tourists would say when they visited my bar." Ramona smiled as she rubbed the back of her head.

"Don't worry, you'll get it down. And hey, now we *both* have something to work on."

The two shared a laugh before Ekchuah called out to them. His voice echoed out of Draco Azul's external speakers.

"Glad you two are having a good time down there, but right now we have a situation on our hands!"

In a few minutes, the two rejoined Ekchuah in the robot's cockpit. There they saw the holographic AI displaying a few projected screens, each depicting various news articles covering the exact same story. One such display featured subtitles directly captioned by Ekchuah himself for Eric's sake.

"On the night we were fighting that Diablo, some nasty business went down at an illegal dog fighting event."

"Dog fighting?" the pilot spoke. "I know it's bad, but why does Draco need to be involved?"

"I was getting to that," Ekchuah replied as he showcased several images of bloodied chalk outlines, blankets, and body bags.

"Dios mío…" Ramona whispered under her breath.

"God, what the hell happened?" asked an equally mortified Eric.

"It gets worse," Ekchuah continued. "The police found the victims' bodies drained of all their blood without any puncture wounds. Their corpses were left as either dried husks or mutilated beyond recognition."

The non-corporeal being's words rang true as the pair stared at the photographed and video-recorded evidence from the news report.

"What could've done this, coach?" Eric queried.

"It certainly wasn't a coyote, I'll tell ya that. But that's not all."

With a wave of his arm, Ekchuah changed the broadcast signal to another news story covering an incident at a very familiar location around an equally recognizable landmark.

"It's the Diablo from Chihuahua City!" Eric blurted out as he witnessed yet another case of multiple homicides. This time, the incident involved the Mexican military and the quarantine zone surrounding Draco Azul's most recent foe. "Jesus, it's another massacre."

"Hold on," said Ramona as she pointed at the screen. "What happened to the Diablo? It's got scratch marks all over it and its skin is all wrinkled."

Eric was so busy looking at the victims that he failed to notice the actual state of the building-sized behemoth. Indeed, its body was covered in lacerations and was now in a dry, shriveled state of decay.

"Neither the military nor government representatives have disclosed what went down last night," the AI explained in a regretful tone. "But from the looks of it, something's been having a helluva feast."

Ekchuah turned away from the screens as he prepared to reveal something to his allies.

"Now, I have my suspicions, but I can't be sure just yet. We're gonna need to investigate."

Ramona stepped up to voice her concerns. "How do we do that?"

"We're gonna need a blood sample from one of those corpses. If it is who I think it is, there's gotta be some trace of it left behind."

"Where do we start, the Diablo?" Eric proposed.

"Naw. It was pretty well guarded before, and now with the breach and this media circus. Also, there's no way we can go in there without Draco, and the last thing we need is any attention on us."

"I see," Eric acknowledged. "Then we hit the first crime scene."

"And if it is who you think it is?" Ramona asked.

Ekchuah stood quiet as he held an expression of great concern.

"Then expect a bloodbath."

***

Later that afternoon, after several hours of trekking from the valley, Eric and Ramona made it back to Chihuahua city. The pair could have made it there quicker had an exhausted Ramona not needed to stop periodically to rest.

"How are you not tired?" questioned Ramona. "We've been walking for a while now!"

"I don't know," Eric replied. "Ever since I started piloting Draco, I don't get exhausted like I used to. Heh, back then I couldn't walk a block without sweatin' up a storm!"

"Hmm, maybe all that time in the robot is finally paying off," Ramona joked.

"Ha, yeah. At least *some* good is coming out of all this." Eric's smile slowly faded as he thought about all the battles that came before and those that are sure to come.

Noticing his shift in mood, Ramona tried to think of another topic that could keep his mind off whatever was pulling him down. It wasn't long until she pointed at her companion's wardrobe.

"So… that coat. How are you not sweating in it?"

"Hm?" Eric looked down at his brown leather duster. "Well, the heat never bothered me. At least, not while wearing this."

He pulled down his sweater to reveal his pilot suit underneath his shirt, a thin, almost spandex-like material that covered his entire body from the neck down save for his hands.

"It seems to keep my body temperature in check. Whenever I train with Ekchuah, I never sweat until after I take off the suit."

"Interesting," Ramona replied. "And what about the coat? Why do you take it everywhere?"

"Oh," Eric was suddenly taken aback. Indeed, he had taken it with him almost every time he went beyond the safety of his mech's cockpit.

"W-well, it used to belong to some folks I knew. They gave it to me as a gift. K-kept it ever since."

Ramona could tell he was growing more uncomfortable as she prolonged the topic. Clearly, she thought, this was a very sensitive subject for her friend. Thankfully, for her sake, she spotted their destination up ahead.

"Hey, there it is! Get ready."

With his mind focused, Eric snapped his attention to the mission at hand.

"Don't gotta tell me twice!"

As the two made a beeline towards the crime scene, they could see a flood of people surrounding the area. Dozens of reporters and bloggers had flocked to the warehouse to capitalize on the attack from the night before. Meanwhile, numerous cops guarded the site by keeping the townsfolk at bay.

"There's gotta be a way to get past these folks," Eric commented.

"Even if we do, we still have to deal with the police. More than likely a few of them are tied to the gangs that hosted their dog fights here. If these cops are like the ones I dealt with back home, then they're probably hiding evidence that could get them in trouble."

"Seriously? It's that bad?"

"They'll do anything for the right price. That's how it's done in this country," Ramona sadly admitted.

Half an hour went by as the crowd began to die down. With the assemblage at a more manageable size, Eric surveyed the scene and noticed the medics transporting the last of the dehydrated cadavers, wrapped in a body bag on a stretcher. At the same time, Ramona could detect the vast amounts of dried blood painted across the front doors of the factory from the horrific odor they gave off.

The reporters began to swarm the medics, demanding their questions be answered.

"What killed these men?"

"Is this going to lead to a gang war?"

"Do you have any leads?"

The police did their best to fend off the parasitic journalists, all while the medics brought the final corpse onboard the ambulance. Ramona and Eric examined the scenario and decided to act.

"Alright, here's the plan," Eric said. "I'll distract the cops by acting as an aggressive reporter. The moment they get their hands on me, you'll wipe the body with this." He pulled out a white cloth to acquire the DNA they needed and passed it to the young lady. "At this point, getting a blood sample from the factory would only give us more trouble than necessary. The place is way too guarded."

"I understand," Ramona replied.

Just as the two were about to set their scheme in motion, a blood-curdling scream erupted from the ambulance, followed immediately by the wet splattering of fluids. The crowd that once enveloped the vehicle began running for their lives in panic. From there, the two witnessed a ghastly sight.

The previously lifeless cadaver was suddenly standing on its own two feet. It hopped out of the medical truck, revealing a string of intestines in its hand. The grisly figure hunched over as it consumed the fresh organs. Behind him, within the ambulance, laid the remains of the medical staff that once tended to the now undead hoodlum.

The macabre gangster's rotting skin began to heal as it absorbed the life-giving nectar that was its victims' blood. As its body rejuvenated, it started to take on an entirely new appearance, one unrecognizable from how it appeared in its previous life.

Hair began growing all over the gangster's body. The ears enlarged and lengthened. Any semblance of a human face vanished as it distorted into a bat-like profile with a grizzly maw and thin, gray skin.

As the former human's body continued its transfiguration, Eric and Romana could hear its bones cracking and realigning. Quickly, the creature's fingers extended. Its skin stretched between each digit; tapering out into large blankets of a thin membrane. Its feet finally burst out of their shoes and transformed into a pair of digitigrade legs. With the metamorphosis complete, the beastly ghoul's head darted around as if it was looking for something.

It wasn't long before it set its pupilless eyes on the remaining crowd that was too afraid to flee. The ghoul spread out its newly formed wings and let out a bestial screech.

CHAPTER 4

Ramona and Eric stood still, terrified as they gazed at the inhuman visage of the bat-like creature. Glowing saliva dripped from the creature's jaws down onto its thin body. Its shaking, frail form was a clear sign that the transmogrified ghoul was in a state of emaciation. The illuminating slobber also indicated the more alarming fact that it was ravenously hungry. The monster leaped into the air and flapped its wings. It let out one last shriek before it began its hunt.

Gunshots rang out and screams were silenced as both civilians and law enforcement attempted, and failed, to evade the winged demon's wrath. Bullets proved useless against the brute's newly strengthened hide as it landed on a random officer before biting down on her neck. After a few seconds of draining the woman's blood, the man-bat swiftly moved on to its next target.

Throats were torn out, rib cages were smashed, and limbs were snapped. All the while, Eric and Ramona were frozen in terror at the nightmare that was once a mortal man.

"En el nombre del Padre, del Hijo, y del Espíritu Santo. Amen."

Upon hearing Ramona reciting the sign of the cross, Eric snapped out of his horrified trance. He grabbed his companion's hand and ran from the carnage as fast as humanly possible.

After claiming a nearby reporter as its fifth victim, the ghoul seemed revitalized. The beast howled triumphantly as its body ceased trembling and its strength was fully restored. Yet, its blood-stained mouth still oozed illuminated spit. The beast's hunger had not yet been soothed. It wasn't long before the bat-like monstrosity finally decided to turn its attention towards the fleeing crowd.

Both Eric and Ramona were caught in a stampede of men and women, all sprinting as fast as their feet could take them. All the while, Eric desperately held his grip on Ramona so as not to lose her in the panicked rush. Ramona, meanwhile, quickly looked behind them to see if the bat-ghoul was flying after them. However, it wasn't flying, nor even running in their direction. It simply stood in place, as if it was waiting for something.

Eric pulled his left arm towards his face, ready to summon his giant mech. All he needed was to recite the three key words into the device to activate Draco Azul and have Ekchuah guide it to his current location. Before he could take such action, however, multiple pairs of hands spewed from the earth below.

What were these creatures? Eric wondered. Are they connected to the bat-beast? How long were they there? It was as though they were bidding their time for their chance to strike once enough victims had gathered, with the bat waiting on the surface. Was there some mastermind behind all of this?

The soil gave way to reveal the humanoids' heads and torsos. Before long, their entire bodies emerged, growling and shrieking in anticipation for the chance to satisfy their unquenchable thirst for blood. The pale figures had cut off most of the escapees from safety as they encircled the group.

With the panicked mob detained, another set of arms burst from the ground and grabbed onto several unfortunate victims, Eric among them. Ramona turned back to see her friend detained by four pale arms that each sprung from beneath the earth.

"Eric!" Ramona screamed out.

Fearing for her safety, Eric let go of Ramona's hand and struggled to pry the devilish limbs that were attached to his legs.

"I got this!" he yelled out to her. "You go help the others!"

Ramona looked around and noticed the zombie-like beings holding onto their victims as they emerged from the soil. She then reached into her pocket and pulled out her stainless steel pocketknife, an item she carried long before she had ever met Eric and Ekchuah. Having been trained by her father's friends in knife combat, it had long since become her preferred weapon against the scum she had come across in her hometown. She sprinted towards the nearest person, a cameraman in his forties, and thrust her blade into one of the two arms that latched onto him.

The young woman could hear the creature wailing in pain before it burst from the ground to attack her. Without so much of a second thought, Ramona impaled the ghoul through the forehead with her knife.

Luckily, the attack was enough to kill the re-animated corpse and save the man, who immediately escaped from the horror that had attacked him. Ramona grimaced as she pulled her blade out of the zombified beast. As the knife exited the creature's emaciated skin, green blood spurt from the wound left in its wake.

She quickly went to aid another bystander. One after another, she freed a handful of men and women alike, this time by slicing off the monsters' frail-looking fingers before going for their skulls. Whatever they were, they seemed a lot weaker than the bat-creature that continued to silently stand by, almost as if it was in a trance state.

Meanwhile, as Ramona came to the civilians' rescue, Eric managed to free himself through sheer brute strength, breaking the last ghoul's wrists in the process. As he tried to regroup with his ally, the ghostly demons from earlier began approaching the freed civilians. The majority however, circled around him and the knife-wielding woman.

"Want this the hard way?" Eric sneered. "Fine, your call!"

Utilizing his months of training, Eric launched an assault on each of his enemies with the same level of strength and speed he applied inside his gigantic metal avatar. He had avoided each of their slow, easily telegraphed swipes, before snapping their brittle limbs and throwing their surprisingly lightweight bodies at each other.

Outside of a few rare occasions. Eric had always tried to keep his newfound combat prowess to an absolute minimum. It was easy for him to get lost in the violence after fighting numerous Diablos for so long. So much so that a part of him feared that he would find himself mistaking a regular person for a monster he would slay any day of the week.

However, the adversaries he was facing were certainly no human beings, at least not any longer. They were cold, merciless monstrosities, thus allowing him the chance to cut loose.

"Heads up! They're coming towards you!" was what Ramona heard from behind as she freed the last person in her vicinity. She then quickly noticed three more monsters slowly approaching her, along with the various fingerless brutes that had already emerged from the ground.

As soon as she saw an opening between her and Eric, Ramona swiftly made a beeline towards him. With each ghoul that confronted her, she would slice them in a sensitive portion of their body in retaliation. One such foe was stabbed in its groin, with another across the eyes. Finally, another had its neck slit, leaving it bleeding profusely. Bringing the pain was one thing the young lady knew how to do quite well.

After a brief period of rest, the bat-creature awoke as it took notice of the disaster that had befallen its fellow beasts. Several had been incapacitated with the remaining few surrounding a pair of relentless humans. The beast took to the air with its sights on the duo. Eric was aghast at seeing the bat-like monstrosity moving once again. Suddenly, one of the ghostly phantoms leaped onto his back, trying to clamp its jaws onto his neck. Fortunately, Ramona made it just in time to deliver a swift strike to the revenant's face.

"Could use some Draco action right now!" Ramona shouted to Eric while she was stomping down on the humanoid's hands.

"I'm working on tha- get down!"

Eric pushed Ramona to the ground, just barely bypassing the bat-creature's grasp as it instead crushed two innocent humans within its brutal claws. The two hastily stood back up and found themselves and the survivors surrounded by an enclosing circle of the undead humanoids. The situation was getting worse, and they both knew it. They couldn't protect everyone nor themselves at that point. Seeing one last opening, Eric activated his DraComm with the utterance of one single phrase:

"Draco Azul, rise!"

Now, all the pilot and Ramona had to do was survive just long enough. Eric could feel his heart beating in his chest, thinking that at any second Draco Azul will appear. He could see the bat-like fiend flying, turning around for another attack as the hoard continued to encompass them.

C'mon! C'mon! Eric thought to himself. Ramona held tightly onto his arm as they both found themselves facing what could be their final moments.

The bat-ghoul readied its claws to ensnare its trapped prey. Right as the flying horror was about to hit its mark, a thunderous noise could be heard from above. Before the demonic figure could check its surroundings, a gigantic metal hand swatted the creature away like it was nothing more than an irritating gnat. This sent the bat-like monstrosity straight into the ground, creating a large crater upon impact. The pilot's hopes were answered as the ground shook beneath himself and his partner.

He noted that the slender life forms at the robot's feet were left dumbstruck by the enormous being. This moment of silence gave the surviving humans the chance to finally flee the vicinity as they all ran past the pale, zombie-like beings. Eric and Ramona set their attention on the bizarre humanoids that remained, ready to board Draco Azul as it placed its massive hand near them.

Then mysteriously, as if on cue, each of the creatures simultaneously hissed and scurried away into the holes they erupted from. In a matter of minutes, they had all vanished into the earth below. Eric and Ramona, both out of breath, took a minute to recuperate.

"That... was way... too close," Ramona said.

"Sorry about that," Eric replied. "I'll try to be quicker next time."

"There's a difference between trying and doing," she reminded Eric.

The two walked over to the crater where the bat-like beast had fallen. To their surprise, despite its bloodied and battered appearance, the winged ghoul was somehow still breathing, if barely. Another revelation was that its blood carried a green luminescence similar to its and the others' saliva.

Eric was in sheer disbelief. While he had faced numerous bizarre entities, this thing was unlike anything he had ever seen. He then looked over to Ramona, who pulled a cloth from her pocket.

"What's that for?" he asked

"I'll head down and get a sample," she replied.

"No, let me. It might be dangerous."

"I'll be fine. You need to check with Ekchuah on how Draco's doing."

The mech pilot was uncomfortable leaving his friend alone with a creature that tore men and women apart like cardboard.

"Don't worry!" Ramona replied, trying to reassure him. "Besides, you get that tech stuff way better than me."

As Ramona flashed a cheeky grin, Eric's concern finally wavered.

"Alright. Just holler if you need anything."

As Eric boarded his mech, the leather jacket-clad woman slowly slid down into the crater, not wanting to make too much noise. The young woman could hear the bat-creature breathing erratically, so she took small steps towards it, looking out for any sudden movements from the monster.

Getting a closer look, she could see the monster's bones were shattered and pierced through its skin. It wasn't going to survive the night, and there was no telling if the others would come back to retrieve their fallen comrade. Whatever might happen to the creature, it was best to obtain whatever DNA samples she could get while it was still alive. Ramona looked down at the cloth in her hand.

Okay, now or never.

The lady slowly placed the cloth on the bat-beast's mouth, slowly wiping a trickle of blood. She was sweating bullets, shaken at the thought of the creature snapping its eyes open at any moment. Finished taking the sample, Ramona just as carefully climbed out of the crater. Once she gave them the okay, she was allowed inside the cockpit where Eric and Ekchuah were waiting. Both could see the obviously relieved look that the young lady was giving them. Ramona walked up to Eric and handed him the DNA sample.

"Don't ever let me do that again."

"Hey, you insisted," Eric chuckled. "Luckily, Ekchuah got most of the repairs done."

"Yup," the hologram confirmed, "everything's working at 95% capacity. All that's needed is a few more hours for the nanomachines to repair the armor. Now let's see what we're dealing with."

Eric placed the tissue in a scanner stationed within the walls of the cockpit. Draco Azul's computer continuously scanned for anything in the beast's DNA that would indicate its origin and composition. After a few minutes of waiting for results, the scans finally developed results. Images of blood cells appeared before the trio as a series of holographic screens. For the pair of humans, this was beyond their scientific comprehension.

"Well, Coach, what do we got?" Eric asked, looking at Ekchuah.

His mentor grew more worried the longer he analyzed the results.

"That bad?"

"More than that, I'm afraid," The hologram stated.

With a simple hand gesture, Ekchuah zoomed in on the blood cells to reveal a spiral-shaped organelle inside its membrane.

"That right there, is a mark of something I wish stayed dead long ago."

"What is it?" Ramona asked.

The AI projected several more screens as he browsed the Internet. Flashes of Mesoamerican imagery flashed before displaying an array of ancient Aztec architecture and paintings. Each one depicted a rather peculiar creature. Next to each image was an article with one word highlighted on each screen.

"Nagual?"

"It's a vampiric creature that shapeshifts into any animal form, as well as humans," Ekchuah explained. "The most notable transformation back in its day was a jaguar. While it shares several traits with European vampires, it's more similar to America's legend of Skinwalkers. Unlike regular vampires, they suck blood through circular marks on their fingers once they dig their claws into their prey. Their fingertips work like how certain animals absorb water through their skin.

"In the past, they were known to infect certain humans with their own blood through the same method, turning them into what you'd call 'ghouls.' Our bat friend down there is one of them. When a human is turned, they crave nothing but blood while also being under the complete control of their creator. By that point, they lose all sense of humanity. What you got left is a mindless and bloodthirsty shell of a human being."

"¡Ay, Dios!" Ramona whispered in horror.

"Hold on, you mean to tell me vampires are real?" Eric questioned.

"Are you really that surprised, kid? After everything we've been through already?"

"No… I guess not. I just hoped we didn't have anything else to worry about beyond the Diablos."

"Trust me," the AI assured his pupil. "Draco was made to fight more than just Diablos. You should know this by now."

"Has Draco ever faced this thing in the past?" queried Ramona.

"We've tried to catch a few in our time," Ekchuah replied, "but they always managed to slip from our grasp. This was an issue the locals usually handled. Eventually, we stopped hearing of them altogether. Your predecessors and I presumed the Naguals either went extinct or had gone into hiding. Obviously, it was the latter."

"We gotta do something," Eric proclaimed. "If these Naguals aren't stopped, all of Mexico will be slaughtered in a few days!"

"Makes sense how they would go after the gangs first since they operate in private," Ekchuah hypothesized. "With an appearance this grand, it seems they're ready to expand their horizon."

"Hmm," Ramona pondered. "Maybe they'll attack another dog fight. The one in Chihuahua should give us a lead on their next target."

Ekchuah immediately opened several holographic screens and scoured the Internet thoroughly to find any information on nearby dog fights. Nothing was coming up, much to his annoyance.

"Not surprised you haven't found anything," sighed Ramona. "They're not just gonna expose themselves online for anybody to see."

"Yeah, well, we need some way of finding them," grumbled Ekchuah. "I'm open to suggestions."

Ramona tried thinking of something, but ultimately drew a blank. Eric, however, was thinking in silence, pondering a place where they could look. Then, an idea lit up in his head… a bad one. Ramona noticed and looked at him with a perplexed expression.

"Hey, you okay?" Ramona asked.

"Try checking the dark web," Eric begrudgingly told Ekchuah as he began searching.

"Wait, what's the-?"

"You don't wanna know," he responded as quickly as she asked. It was clear she did not spend enough time online to learn of the existence of the disgusting portion of the Internet that housed some of the most depraved actions mankind could achieve.

Checking through the dark web in private so as not to disturb his teammates, Ekchuah finally picked up the data they needed for upcoming dog fights. The biggest one that was scheduled to occur was in an abandoned mining town called Ojuela.

"Okay, we'll head to Ojuelo," the AI decided. "Once there, we'll go undercover and hope the ghouls strike. When they do, we'll find and kill the leader."

"They have leaders?" Eric asked.

"Of course. It's clear there's one or several who's infecting regular people and turning them into lesser Naguals, those pale ones who you guys were fighting. Only a pure Nagual, one that isn't human, can turn others into similar beings, but not exactly like them. From what we've gathered over the centuries, once they're taken out, their ghouls should either revert to normal or die."

Ramona was shocked by that last bit, hoping there would be no casualties by the end of this nightmare.

"Wait! There's a chance we can't cure these people?" she objected.

"How the Naguals work is still a mystery, as it tends to be on a case-by-case basis with their followers," the hologram explained. "It might depend on the strength of each Nagual and their control over their respective ghouls, but it's only a theory."

While saddened by the revelation, Ramona knew Ekchuah was right. While it was preferable if they tried to save those infected, it was better in the long run for these ghoulish monstrosities to die before they could harm any more innocent lives, as she witnessed firsthand.

"Does this mean we have to…?" she trailed off before she could finish as she stared at a monitor displaying the feeble beast.

"Sorry," Ekchuah answered. "It's the only way."

By now, Eric had changed into his pilot gear and stepped into the ring that allowed him full control of Draco Azul.

"I'll handle this. As long as those Naguals are out there, any amount of time this creature lives poses a grave threat to everyone."

As he prepared to stomp the creature to death, the mech's extrasensory vision detected no life signs from the still body of the broken monster. The creature had already perished. Realizing that it at one point had been human, the pilot decided that the being deserved a human funeral at the very least.

He manipulated his giant robot to grab a hold of the corpse, raised it to the mech's chest, and discharged a small portion of lightning from its horn. With the corpse obliterated, Eric gently spread the ashes towards the nearby ocean.

This wasn't a makeshift ritual for just one individual, however. It was for every single victim whose lives have been forever silenced by such a heinous villain, one that the young man swore he would bring an end to.

CHAPTER 5

Inside one of the many abandoned buildings within the dilapidated town of Ojuela, restless corpse-like figures were clawing at the ground, screaming into the air, and biting their own arms and legs. Desperately trying to draw blood from themselves and each other, the twenty-five ghouls were starving after their failed attack on the humans earlier that day. Had it not been for the appearance of the blue metal giant, they would have had enough nourishment to survive the next two days. Before they could cause any further harm to each other, the front door slowly opened to reveal their overseer, the Dogman that attacked the gang near Chihuahua City. As the Dogman gazed into their empty stares, he could clearly see that all of them needed more blood. Luckily for them, he was more than happy to oblige.

"Sorry for taking so long, but I got dinner!" he said to everyone in what used to be their native language prior to their transformations.

However, none of them were paying any mind to their caretaker as they slowly returned to attacking each other like rabid animals. Despite this, the Dogman walked back outside to bring in the several corpses he acquired during his hunt. These unfortunate victims were once tourists exploring the remains of the ghost town that was their current base of operations. What was once a bustling mining village, Ojuela deteriorated into a shadow of its former self once its natural resources were picked clean. Until the arrival of the vampiric menace and his cohorts, the desolate center was only ever visited by travelers with an appreciation for history.

The Dogman made sure to acquire enough casualties to feed everyone. He threw all five of the corpses on the floor, one after the other. Once the bodies made impact, his followers leaped towards their meals. The revenants tried to suck the blood from the fresh husks, yet it wasn't enough to satiate all of them. Quickly, the ghouls turned on each other once again.

"Hey! Hey! Hey! No fighting!" The Dogman shouted.

The keeper of the ghouls forced himself into the middle of the crowd, trying to prevent further conflict. This led to some of his own kinfolk slashing and smacking his face, torso, and limbs. Frustrated by his inability to control them, he let loose an unnerving and unnatural shriek that managed to scare every one of them into hiding. The Dogman sighed as he was finally able to get some form of tranquility.

"I'm sorry," the ringmaster apologized, *"I just want everyone to get along."*

The Dogman walked around, staring at all his followers, or what he viewed as "family." To him, they were the closest thing he had to one.

Suddenly one of the male followers spoke out loud, an ability ghouls were normally incapable of accomplishing.

"We are immortals!" he proclaimed. These ghouls wore the tattered remains of a buttoned dress shirt and slacks. The speaker in particular was one of the gangsters that was converted by the Dogman rather than slain that night. *"Impossible to kill by any human! Why not strike now?"*

"I concur," a teenage male ghoul agreed. *"But we are not dealing with any ordinary threat. As long as the giant stands in our way, we are helpless. It made quick work of the Diablo we feasted on. Also, our numbers are still low. We need more additions to the family."*

Behind the two individuals, the Dogman's hands were raised, each palm illuminating a bright green glow. He was twitching his fingers anytime each of them spoke or made the smallest of gestures. He was a puppeteer, simulating a conversation by projecting false words, thoughts, and emotions into the speakers to give the illusion that they were intelligent beings capable of speech. To stave off his crippling isolation, their creator took to creating mock discussions between him and his followers. As he began these sessions of role-playing, he deluded himself into thinking the ghouls were just as sentient as he was. To him, they were more than mere mindless minions. They were just like him.

The Dogman pointed his other hand at a feeding female, who began to stand upright.

"He is right!" she spoke with blood trickling down her mouth. *"We've been hiding in the shadows for centuries. To attempt an uprising requires absolute cautiousness."*

"Yes," replied the first ghoul in the tattered suit. *"That is how we've been able to hide for centuries. And that's exactly why we need to act now. Bring extinction to the humans before they can hunt us down first!"*

"You imbecile!" shrieked the female follower. *"There's no need to go that far."*

Suddenly, the teenager intervened once again. *"Indeed. We just need a city to thrive in and plenty of sustenance-"*

"Human blood is the only 'sustenance' we need to keep us alive!" the aggressive inhuman spouted as he interrupted his younger counterpart. *"Making peace with our food is completely insane!"*

All three then turned toward the Dogman, as if looking to him for guidance. In reality, he had simply pulled his hands in to bring all three of his flesh puppets closer to him. As he made his followers argue amongst each other, he was in actuality debating with himself on what direction he would move forward with. Each figure represented a potential decision he could make.

He stuttered in giving an answer to his proxies, participating in the false conversation with feigned humbleness.

"Why must you always turn to me for answers? I'd rather hear what all of you have to say."

"Don't be so modest, dear leader," the female retorted.

52

"You always know the right thing to do," the suited one added.

"After all," retorted the adolescent, *"as the oldest, you've learned more of what mankind is capable of than anyone else here."*

"Yes," the female ghoul spoke up once more. *"You've taught us how humans may seem friendly, but they have always hunted our kind down."*

"Lastly," said the teen. *"They've only ever referred to you as 'Nagual' once you became the last of our kind. It's been so long since you've been called anything else that you can't even recall your true name."*

The male ghoul stepped towards the Dogman in confidence. *"Now it is time for us to be the hunters, not the hunted."*

"Dinner!" The caretaker abruptly spurted. In response, he made all three appear as if they were all caught off guard.

"Would any of you want seconds? I just remembered I had one more body outside." The Dogman went back out, only to carry in an extremely obese dead man with ease. Immediately, all the followers drooled and hissed in response, no longer under his control.

"Okay! Okay! Fine. Be done in a few minutes. This one needs a little prep work."

The ghouls' keeper took the bloated corpse into the kitchen. While many humans were turned into undead figures like him, the vampiric creature captured others simply for nourishment to feed both himself and his faux brethren. Tonight, he was planning to give each of them giant buckets of blood fit for a king. The Dogman extended his claws and sunk them into the cadaver's torso and ripped it wide open before drawing out its red liquid.

He poured the crimson nectar into multiple buckets until each one was full. Some would be used for tonight, while others would be saved for later. These containers were placed in a corner of the room where samples of the Diablo's blood were stored.

As he prepared his family's meal, he inspected the body and found a wallet in its back pocket. He peered into the item and found a photo of what appeared to be the same man with his family, all smiling over a large Christmas dinner. The chicken looked piping hot, right out of the oven. Memories flashed through the Dogman's mind of the times when the last Nagual was all alone, struggling to survive. The humans pursued him like an animal, viewing him as nothing more than a monster despite his attempts to avoid consuming humans at all costs. He and his people had learned to hate humanity more than they feared them.

Further memories emerged, ones of the Nagual spending decades in hibernation through forced starvation, only to awaken when in desperate need of food. During these brief moments when he would pursue nourishment would he oversee mankind from the shadows. Multiple times the Nagual caught humans enjoying the comforts of family and especially the variety of food their bodies could enjoy. As delicious as they may have seemed to the silent stalker, he could never enjoy either luxury.

"Thus, the pitfalls of my kind. Always needing to survive on plasma, never allowing ourselves the chance to surpass beyond our physical limitations. Yet, it is what it is," the Dogman spoke out loud.

He noticed the collected buckets becoming full of enough fluid to energize his companions. However, an idea took shape in the man's head on how he could prepare a different kind of meal and perhaps introduce it to the others.

"Hmmm, maybe I could add a bit more flavor to it."

He placed the buckets on a rusty old stove, trying his best to light it up. Failing a couple of times, the revenant had to be careful with the leaking gas as he didn't want to set anything ablaze.

Finally, after a few attempts, he was able to get the stoves working and placed one bucket on it. As the Dogman waited for the blood to boil, his thoughts referred to the early "conversation" with his three family members. Each had brought up solid points.

The Nagual had been hunted down by mankind for centuries and it was time to fight back. However, at the same time, he had seen humans treat each other with kindness.

Could it be that he approached them incorrectly? He recalled being referred to as a monstrosity, and of course, the name that he had since adopted. While it was something he never chose to embrace, the title of "Nagual," roughly translating to "transforming witch," stuck around long enough to where it was the closest thing he had to an identity. This became distressingly apparent as time passed and his species was relegated to mere legends of shapeshifting spirits. The Nagual realized then that he must declare war on humanity, as they had their chance and failed dreadfully. He now had a brood that needed him and there was no turning back.

A few more minutes passed, and the blood was now boiling. The Dogman pulled out a dirty old spoon and took a sample of the heated plasma. After fanning the blood, he poured it into his mouth. The inhuman creature's ability to live off blood enabled him to feel the fluid's taste, texture, and temperature. With this information in mind, the caretaker loved the sensation of warm blood.

This added care to the life-giving nectar provided it with an extra flavor that was exquisite. The divine sensation of ingesting his creation enticed the monster into indulging himself with a second spoonful of the concoction. He stopped as he realized that this was not for himself since there were over two dozen of his companions waiting in the main hall for their promised meal.

Back outside, the others were getting restless, yet the smell of fresh blood kept them at bay… for the moment, at least. Finally, the Dogman carried out several buckets of blood onto the dining room table. The corpses slowly approached the scarlet fluid. They sniffed the air when they sensed the blood was different from how it usually smelled.

This time it was warm, like the sun that scorched above. Regardless of the scent, blood was still blood. After a few minutes, their overseer carried out the last of the buckets.

"Dinner's ready!" he said proudly.

Hunger drove all of them. Every single one of the followers jumped over each other to absorb the blood that their bodies desperately needed.

"Hold it!"

All the revenants looked towards him as he wore a disapproving brow over its eyes. His face then shifted from serious to cheerful.

"We must say grace before eating! So, let's all sit first and not act like animals."

With a wave of the Dogman's hands, everyone simultaneously looked down at the chairs in front of them and acted on command, sitting as if they were still the humans they once were. The Dogman took the head of the table where he began to utter a prayer:

"We thank our ancestors for this wonderful feast, may we continue to thrive. And hope that one day we may find pe-"

Before he could finish, everyone began feeding to their insatiable hearts' content. The caretaker sighed in disappointment. He could not complete his short prayer, though it couldn't be helped. Centuries ago, the Nagual culture had deteriorated to the point where their kind sacrificed almost everything for the sake of their own survival. He believed that manners were one of those casualties.

Still, it didn't mean that he couldn't find out what everyone thought of his "cooking," as it were. The Dogman stood up and walked around his followers, watching all of them enjoying their meals.

"Hmm?" a revenant said to herself as she slurped her meal. Once again, her caregiver was doing the speaking for her.

"How's it taste?" Nagual asked eagerly to his "relative."

"Pretty good, but it's lacking texture. And your heating of the fluid leaves a lot to be desired."

The Dogman's visage furrowed. He acted offended that anyone would feel that way towards his first attempt at preparing a meal. In truth, being considerate and merciful was not the persona she was assigned.

"Eh, everybody's a critic," he begrudgingly replied back.

Despite that one little complaint, everyone else seemed to love their meal. Though the Dogman only assumed so as he chose not to create another pseudo-conversation with any of his followers. He walked back to his table and finished drinking all the blood from his bucket, seemingly enjoying every bit of the experience.

Just then, the Calupoh that had accompanied him earlier arrived at the front door. It had returned after surveying the land for any would-be intruders. Its return meant that the canine had not found anyone yet. With the coast clear, it was time for Dogman to head out. While he would rather take the time to slowly enjoy his meal like everyone else, there was still a job to do. As the guardian of this new family unit, it was his duty to expand their ranks.

The blood drinker walked towards the nearest window to once again look out in the direction of the gorgeous city of Durango. No matter what, the sight of the centuries-old constructions of man was always a sight to behold, especially via his enhanced telescopic vision.

Untouched by the sands of time was the building the Nagual always admired, the Cathedral Basilica. He was never sure why he always gravitated towards churches. Perhaps it was the architectures that were beautifully made by human standards. It could've been how these buildings represented the hopes and prayers of all who entered their hallowed doors. Maybe they were always the means of bringing families together. The Nagual was fully aware of the humans' ritual of bonding through their united love of religion. This was a puzzle the Nagual could never figure out.

Just then, a memory latched onto the Dogman's mind and drew his attention away from the here and now. He could see it in vivid detail. One summer night many years ago, the Nagual had perched himself upon the roof of a cathedral in a small town. Looking down to the streets below, he witnessed a pair of women with two small boys happily running and playing nearby. The pale phantom was not sure if the women were best friends, neighbors, or family. His best guess was that they were close.

In the present day, the Dogman looked back to the brood. Everyone was full from the blood they had consumed. Soon, they all crawled into their corners to rest for a quick nap.

Hope sooner or later I can get at least a sentence out of everyone, he thought to himself.

It had been frustrating for the Nagual that his family was acting in such a feral manner. Without his help, they were nothing like his fully sentient brethren from days past. He hoped they could catch up to his lost relatives in due time. If not, then it was going to be an arduous task teaching them how to speak, one the exhausted specter was certainly not going to enjoy. In the meantime, it was time to increase the size of his family.

He looked over to the Calupoh, currently waiting for him.

"Okay everyone, we'll be back in a few hours. Oh, and do feel free to join in on the fun later. Going to be hosting a big party later on and you're all invited!"

His farewell fell on deaf ears as everyone had fallen asleep. The Dogman shrugged this off and left with his canine partner following right alongside him.

CHAPTER 6

As darkness enveloped the sky, a crowd gathered under an old, abandoned suspension bridge, a symbol of the once-populated town of Ojuela. While it had been a tourist attraction since the late 20th century, it was now a breeding ground for a new dog fighting tournament. Gang members from around Durango state had arrived for wealth, fame, and power. Among these dangerous individuals stood one lone woman who tried her best to blend into the crowd. It was Ramona, donning her father's jacket as she was next in line at the security check.

"You here to compete or watch?" questioned one of the five bodyguards.

"Just here for the show," Ramona answered in an aggressive tone.

"Who are you representing?" another guard asked.

"Los Gigantes."

"The what?"

Upon being asked, Ramona turned and showed off the back of her father's jacket. Embroidered on it was the illustration of a demon surrounded by fire. Underneath it was a banner with her father's nickname inscribed on it: "Gigante."

"Oh yeah, Los Gigantes. I thought you guys retired. Not here to start trouble, are ya?"

"You're kidding, right? Start something with all you guys? What do you think I am, stupid?" Ramona replied, acting almost offended that she even needed to answer.

"Any weapons on ya?"

In response, the woman took out her knife and performed a little trick as she flipped it in the air before handing it to a large man.

"Impressive. Doesn't look too dangerous. Alright, you're free to enter."

Ramona said nothing as she got her knife back and entered the area. She had spent enough time with her father, known locally as El Gigante, and his gang, Los Gigantes, to get a sense of how things went down between gangs. While many of them had been dangerous, her father's had been the vigilante type, often keeping scum out of their city for as long as they could. Even after El Gigante's unfortunate death during one particular confrontation, she continued to learn how to defend herself on the streets thanks to her uncle, her father's brother and second-in-command of their posse prior to their eventual breakup.

The idea of going undercover was something she thought she would never have to perform. However, desperate times called for desperate measures, regardless of the risk. Ekchuah sure as hell couldn't go in and Eric had to pilot Draco Azul if another crazy vampire attack were to take place. With all that in mind, Ramona came to this decision several hours prior to her arrival.

***

"If that's the case, then I'll go!" Ramona announced. Both Eric and Ekchuah were in shock at their friend's declaration.

"Absolutely not." Ekchuah sternly objected.

"Look, Ramona, we know you can kick any one of those punks into next week," Eric said. "But with something like the Nagual, it's too much of a gamble. I'll go."

"No. *You* going would be a gamble," Ramona countered. "You've got more responsibilities here. Who's going to pilot Draco if anything happens to you?"

Eric thought for a moment and realized that Ramona did have a valid point. Draco Azul's arrival last time was far too close of a call. Had it taken another minute to arrive they would have been goners. If things were going to get bad, which he felt they were, then they needed Draco Azul on the scene as soon as possible, and Ekchuah's autopiloting could only get them so far.

"And besides, let's remember which one of us is *fluent* in Spanish," Ramona added.

Eric's eyes widened. Ramona was right on the money with that fact. If he went down there, he would stick out like a sore thumb with his limited knowledge of the language and culture.

"She has a point."

Even Ekchuah understood she was right. With everything going on with Diablos, the AI never had time to help Eric learn the Spanish language more efficiently, as it was never a priority.

"Alright, you win," Eric admitted in defeat.

"Eric, hand her the DraComm," ordered Ekchuah before turning to face Ramona. "We'll be monitoring you at all times. We will be close by if things go south."

Ramona nodded. "Deal."

***

Once Ramona entered the gangs' makeshift establishment, she observed her surroundings. She beheld what looked like a flea market from Hell as the area was populated with vendors that sold drugs, guns, and knives.

Within the filthy gathering of degeneracy, a battle was about to begin. In the outdoor ring were two pit bulls. One of them was jet black. He looked to be a very old mutt. If Ramona had to guess, maybe around nine to ten years old. However, the canine had multiple battle scars on his body, a clear veteran of several fights. The other dog was tan with white patches and had the most supporters.

"Is that the reigning champion?" she asked a random attendee covered head to toe in tattoos.

"Of course, babe!" The loud, inebriated man spoke. *"That's Asesino!"*

Upon further investigation, she noticed that Asesino had pronounced muscles and a larger set of teeth than any pit bull she had ever seen. Each hound waited by their owners, patiently standing until the fight was to commence.

"And begin!" the announcer said.

With the foghorn blown, the match began.

The two dogs maimed each other for the twisted amusement of the surrounding men and women. Dozens of men and women all waved cash and screamed for their choice of animal to be the winner. Ramona looked on in disgust, feeling sorry for what these poor creatures were forced into. The young woman wondered what kind of person someone had to be to partake in such a so-called sport. She presumed it would have to be the kind of people who enjoyed inflicting pain onto weaker beings, those who were incapable of understanding the value of life, be it man or beast.

"Horrible, isn't it?" a voice asked from behind Ramona.

Shocked, she turned around with her hand near her pocket. Her eyes met those of a handler with his own canine. However, unlike other dog men who would bring pit bulls, he had a black Calupoh. It was a local breed, but one not used for these fights. The man himself didn't really match the description of your typical gangster.

He was a middle-aged man who was a little scruffy, had a bit of dirt on his clothes and face, and there were two tattoos on his forearm. One with the words *"Family is Forever"* inscribed on his skin in Spanish in an old English font. The other was of an Aztec-style skull. Ramona kept her guard up. If there was anything that she learned from her father, it was that looks could always be deceiving.

"What do you mean?" Ramona remarked as she attempted to mask her anger so as not to sound out of place. The last thing she needed was to blow her cover.

"You need not hide your true feelings," the Dogman said. *"This is an appalling visual. Trust me, I despise this just as much as you do. Humans are a cruel bunch. Never offering a hand or taking a moment to second guess their actions."*

His Calupoh panted and sat right next to the oddly relaxed individual, watching the action alongside his master. Unlike everyone else, this man gave off a seemingly unthreatening aura. Even the tone in his voice was friendly and almost inviting. She could at least agree with this strange person that what they were watching was repulsive. However, if he truly felt this way, why bring his dog here if not to throw his canine into the mix?

"Sounds a bit hypocritical if you're bringing your dog here," Ramona accused as she stared him right in the eyes.

The Dogman chuckled. *"That's not my intention here. I'm going to free every single one of those poor creatures and make these people realize the error of their warped ways."*

At that moment, the stranger's entire demeanor suddenly shifted. The man clenched his fist tightly as he furiously gazed at the horror that was unfolding. Back in the pit, Asesino had the upper hand on the bloodied challenger.

"And how do you intend to do that?" Ramona cautiously asked, seeing the righteous fury in the man's eyes.

"By making everyone see the light."

"And the winner, Asesino!" the host yelled out.

Ramona heard a mix of cheers and boos from the audience over the winning canine. The Dogman smirked as he walked towards the area with his scruffy, pitch-black dog following right behind him. Ramona was puzzled by this pairing. What could they do to make all of this savagery end? If anything, they were going to be ripped apart by everyone. She couldn't let that happen, but at the same time Ramona had to keep a low profile until she could find anything suspicious involving those vampires. She trailed them as they got closer to the pit.

"So, who here thinks they can handle the mighty Asesino?!" the host screamed out to the audience, looking for any takers.

This host had long red hair that flowed over his shoulder and wore a goatee. He was dressed in a black hoodie but had a buttoned-down shirt and cargo pants. Ramona, now shoved between two rowdy onlookers at the edge of the ring, watched on thinking this host had the worst taste in fashion.

"How about something a little different?" the familiar voice of the Dogman said loudly.

Everyone looked back at the man and his Calupoh companion. The host and everyone in the room erupted with laughter at this newcomer and his dog's unassuming appearance. He looked to be no challenge whatsoever.

"Who invited the hobo and his flea-ridden mutt!" Ramona overheard from a nearby woman.

Everyone continued to mock the two. The daughter of Gigante watched on, still in confusion over why he would answer this challenge.

Whatever he has planned, he better make it worthwhile for the audience, for his and the dog's sake, Ramona thought to herself.

"Can that scrawny pooch even fetch a stick?" a man across the ring bellowed, creating a chain of further uproar.

"Listen here, grandpa," a random gangster demanded as he walked up to the Dogman. *"If you know what's best for you, then you'll leave now. Pretend you never saw us. Unless you and your pooch wanna be the appetizers for our hungry fighters?"*

Everyone started surrounding him, switchblades at the ready. The pit bulls that were not in the ring barked and growled, drooling with saliva. These hounds were ready to sink their teeth into something with meat and bones. Smirking, the Dogman looked around at all the gang members.

"There's no need for an altercation. All I'm asking is for you to humor me. I bet my little friend here can take out any of your furry friends in very little time," the Dogman proclaimed very calmly.

Ramona thought it was astonishing that this guy was not soiling himself in fear. He acted so angry one second, then calm and confident the next. Something was definitely wrong.

"You're asking for trouble, idiot!" one woman cried, very enraged by his arrogant comment.

"I don't just want to take up the challenge. At best, you get to see my so-called pooch get ripped to shreds and then do what you will with me. At worst, you'll get an unpredictable winner that could make you guys a lot of money."

No one was buying it, though, and the gathered criminals closed in for the kill. Ramona couldn't stand there and do nothing. This old man might be crazy, but that did not mean he deserved to be murdered.

"Wait!" the host shouted. Everyone stared at him in surprise. *"Let's humor him. You think that living shag carpet can take out every single competitor here?"*

"That's right."

"You got moxie, you old geezer. Alright! So, the great Asesino will go up against the scrawny Calupoh! Place your bets!"

The Dogman walked into the arena while everyone shouted and booed at him. It was a one-sided bet with the only person who believed that the Calupoh would win being his owner. The Calupoh walked into the area, still panting almost like he was cheerfully oblivious to what was about to take place. His pit bull counterpart growled viciously at his new opponent. All the gangsters waved and chanted for Asesino.

Suddenly, the sounds of inorganic screams echoed throughout the valley. Everyone got themselves ready for the worse, each taking out their weapon of choice. Prior to their gathering, the hoodlums all heard rumors of a massacre that went down at another dogfight by some vicious animal. They all believed they were ready for whatever came their way. However, only Ramona knew just how truly terrifying the threat was.

At that moment, dozens of the Nagual's minions burst from the ground and attacked any nearby gangsters they could latch themselves onto. As the bloodthirsty creatures feasted, the remaining thugs tried to fight back. They stabbed and shot their monstrous counterparts with every weapon at their disposal.

Despite their efforts, they were all easily overpowered by the size of the horde. The host himself tried to escape but was forcefully grabbed and thrown to the ground by the Dogman. Ramona's eyes darted all around at the carnage that was unfolding. She activated the DracoComm to call for Eric.

"Eric, the situation's really bad! Get here no-"

Before Ramona could finish her sentence, a pair of ghouls attempted to get the drop on her by attacking from behind. Luckily for her, she could hear their incessant panting and growling. Without hesitation, the young woman punched one in the face, followed by a swift kick to the other's cranium. With her foes dazed, she looked around for a weapon, to which she found a rusty lead pipe buried in the ground.

As Ramona tugged at the piece of decayed metal, three more of the Nagual's minions charged at her. Finally, the young woman broke off a portion of the rotted plumbing as long as a sword. She instinctively swung at the vile fiends like a baseball player up to bat. Utilizing her strength and agility to her advantage, she threw several more kicks to knock her enemies off their feet before smashing their heads in for good measure.

As the warrior woman fought, she could clearly see what Ekchuah meant when he said they needed to eliminate every one of the bloodthirsty vampires. It didn't matter that they were once human. Now, they were nothing more than monsters, creatures as dangerous as the Diablos Draco Azul regularly fought.

While she fended off the ghouls, she heard a haunting voice.

"I told you…"

Ramona looked around, only to find more speechless zombies. Once her eyes caught sight of the Calupoh, still panting in the ring, she started noticing the surrounding creatures stopping in place. She turned her attention back towards the dog and was shocked when the canine slowly melted into a sickening puddle of blackened organs, flesh, and bodily fluids. In mere seconds, the ebony puddle then reconstituted itself into a new humanoid form.

Its new body was bone white, its skin adorned with grey and black tribal-like markings. The being's slender forearms and calves had gaping holes akin to the bones on human limbs. Atop its green-eyed, mouthless cranium were two swept-back spiked protrusions. Finally, at the center of the creature's chest was a blood-red piece of armor that seemed to resemble a heart. This unearthly abomination was the true form of the Nagual.

His otherworldly feline-like eyes stared directly at Ramona. The gaze of the unknown being pierced her soul, petrifying her where she stood. It was through this glare that she suddenly found herself in a sea of emotions.

However, they were not hers. She experienced waves of anger, hatred, and fear. Among such bleak and nihilistic thoughts, one emotion stood out: sorrow. Were these the inner thoughts of the Nagual? Ramona then saw a vision. One of a foreign surreal world and what looked like other Naguals running for their lives. The vision and emotions subsided as the alien raised its left hand outward, revealing spiral-shaped curricular patterns on each of its fingertips.

"They would see things my way," spoke the same voice, this time out loud, as if it was finishing the first entity's sentence mere moments ago. It was the Dogman, walking towards Ramona as he bypassed the frozen minions. However, his body jerked and twitched unnaturally, like someone was manipulating his actions like a marionette.

Ramona noticed then that the Nagual was mirroring the Dogman's hand gestures and body movements perfectly. *What's going on?* she thought.

Even more bizarre was how she heard the same voice from two sources, one from the Dogman and the other one racking around in her brain. The being she presumed was the Nagual had no visible mouth, so Ramona figured it was using some kind of telepathic ability.

Reality set in when she was grabbed from behind by a pair of her enemy's followers. Ramona struggled to break free as best she could. A swift kick to one of her captor's legs set her loose. Fortunately for her these beasts, while savage, had proven to be rather frail and brittle.

Without warning, a massive screech could be heard from on high. It was as loud as thunder and fierce as lightning. It took no time at all for the faux gangster to realize that Eric made it in time with Draco Azul.

"Now, you're finished!" she snarkily remarked to the alien.

Yet, for whatever reason it remained unfazed.

The gargantuan titan landed down on all the ghouls in sight, making sure to leave Ramona and any remaining humans unscathed. Some of the monsters managed to avoid the debris as others got crushed in a gory display. Blood and guts splattered all over the concrete and the robot's metal plating. Draco Azul's scarlet cloth swung down to grab Ramona, shielding her from pieces of rubble that flew into the air during the mech's landing. Quickly, she was lifted into the air and towards the cockpit.

Ramona smiled in gratitude at Draco Azul for saving her life. Gently, she was pushed towards the entrance of the cockpit before she jumped in. Waiting for her were Ekchuah and Eric, who was in his battle suit, ready for the fight ahead of them.

"Thanks for the save."

The pilot in turn gave the thumbs up and braced for battle.

"You alright?" Eric asked.

At first, Ramona didn't answer, still reeling from her encounter with the Nagual.

"Ramona!" Ekchuah called out to her, snapping her back to reality.

"Y-yes, I'm fine," she answered so as not to make her friends worry.

"Good to hear," the hologram responded.

"I'll say," the young man followed up.

Both Eric and Ekchuah nevertheless spotted the contemplative pause on Ramona's face. The encounter with the Nagual had indeed shaken the woman to her very core. As concerned as she was over the actual meaning of that mental link with the Nagual, those thoughts would all have to be put away for now. They had a war to win.

CHAPTER 7

The Nagual gazed up at the mighty form of Draco Azul. Centuries ago, he had but mere glimpses of the giant metal warrior from the stars who faced various gods and monsters beyond the vampire's league. Such destructive power was something he would never have dreamed of ever challenging. During this period, he and his kind had gone to great lengths to evade the azure titan's wrath. Now, hundreds of years later, it stood before him once again, the very same guardian that shook his world before and has done so yet again.

The sound of whimpers caught the vampire-like being's attention. To his horror, several of his family members had been crushed, a sight which caused the Nagual to rush towards them, followed by a few of his other followers that survived the impact. It took the vampiric extraterrestrial all his considerable strength to free his brethren from the chunks of wreckage, only he was too late.

He shook his head in abject disbelief as he laid his eyes upon the slaughtered remains of his newly formed family. The Nagual surveyed the devastation around him and was overwhelmed by the sheer number of his children that had been slain in a single act. All he could do was utter a silent prayer, something he picked up from humans when they honored their deceased loved ones.

This caused the Nagual to clench his fist, never having felt such intense rage or sorrow since he first arrived on this planet. From the time he had first come to this blue orb, he had been treated like a common animal. His sense of connection to anything in this world was tenuous as he had lost his original family long ago. Now, with so many of his clan exterminated, any sympathy, compassion, or mercy he had left within him towards Earth's inhabitants was gone.

He silently decreed that the two humans who had brought this suffering upon him would pay greatly for this injustice, he thought. The remaining ghouls hissed at Draco Azul, recognizing their nemesis from last time, while the Nagual picked himself up and cleared his emotions. He may have lost a sizable chunk of family members, but he needed to keep the majority alive. Fortunately, not only did his brood convert dozens more gang members into fellow ghouls, but the bloodsucker from another world also had a trick up his sleeve. When he and his followers tasted the blood of the Diablo, their increase in strength and endurance were not the only gifts they obtained. The alien vampire addressed his followers.

Fear not, my brethren, the Nagual telepathically told his followers. *We can fight them on the same level. Remember, you drank from the nectar of life. Now, we can transcend to the next level of evolution. Allow one of the strongest to make an example of this tin can.*

He focused on the Dogman, his very first apostle, as through him he had gained so much. To the Nagual leader, this former homeless man was the closest thing he had to a second-in-command or best friend, despite the individual having no more sentience than any other drone. Through the manipulation of the drunkard's blood, the alien managed to craft a being that could maintain his form in contrast to the pale and frail minions that followed.

The Dogman smiled, a reflection of the eagerness barely contained in the Nagual. As green mucus driveled out of his mouth, the ghoul's body began to twitch and convulse, forcibly changing in shape. His hands gained large claws, his skull expanded, his teeth sharpened, and his skin began to grow fur. Whatever clothes remained intact on the Dogman after Draco Azul's arrival ripped off as he morphed into a wolf-like creature. His grotesque features resembled the ungodly combination of a human man and a Mexican wolf. Once the ghoul had completed his transformation, his body began to grow in mass, matching that of the metal giant.

"What the hell?" were the only words that could escape Eric's mouth as he and his team were left completely aghast at this disturbing revelation.

Meanwhile, the Nagual gazed up at his creation in wide-eyed wonder. Had he been born with a mouth, he would be wearing the proudest smile. His minions all backed away from the wolf beast, deeming it another threat. Then the Nagual spoke to his progeny.

"There is nothing to fear! What you see is the pinnacle of our might. In due time, you too will be capable of obtaining such power! For now, keep the mech distracted and pay attention to what our champion can do."

The ghouls hissed before they too transformed at the whim of their master, developing feathered wings from their upper limbs and curved talons from their feet. They had become seven-foot tall, owl-like creatures, as large as the humanoid bat monster from before. These feather-covered creatures screeched loudly and took flight as soon as the Nagual raised his arms as a maestro would conduct an orchestra. Within the Primal Warrior's cockpit, Eric and the others took notice of the mob of monsters soaring towards them.

"Brace yourselves!" Eric yelled to Ramona and Ekchuah.

Draco Azul crossed its arm in anticipation for the impact as the flock of owl-men encircled the mech, scratching, clawing, and pecking at the armor in search of vulnerable points to exploit. Eric directed the mech to swipe at whatever avian ghouls it could get its colossal hands on. The pilot's best attempts were cut short when the giant lycanthrope's elbow thrusted into the armored soldier's chest. Draco Azul, reeling from the offense, countered by delivering a swift strike to the gargantuan Dogman's face.

The werewolf-like creature dodged the punch and pounced on his opponent, only to be stopped by a flowing crimson scarf emanating from the blue colossus. Eric had his mechanical doppelganger grab its cloth and spin the ghoul around three times before throwing it into the nearby plains. The wolf crashed into the ground, landing on his back. Seizing the opportunity, Draco Azul marched towards the Dogman, twirling its scarf as a lasso. As the lycanthrope recovered from its thrashing, he sensed the assault coming this time. With unbelievable timing, the monster bit the scarf, pulling on it to draw Draco Azul closer towards him.

"Oh no you don't, Fido!" Eric remarked as he struggled to regain his weapon.

The Dogman responded by hopping off the ground, thrusting his feet forward, and laying a drop-kick to the robot's head, forcing it to the ground.

"You kids, alright?" a worried Ekchuah asked the jostled Eric and Ramona.

"I'm fine," answered the still-seated woman as she held onto her head. "The straps still work."

"I'm okay as well," a disgruntled Eric responded as he attempted to get back on his feet.

"But he sure ain- gah!"

At that moment, the canine-esque creature jumped on the mechanical giant's back and clawed away at its metallic hull, leaving deep gashes across its armored plating. The ghoul continued the onslaught by chomping down on the machine's left shoulder. As it continued to pin down the humans' metal avatar, dozens of owl-men gathered around the dented portions of the robot's armor and furthered the damage.

Catching the right opportunity, the Nagual's alien form melted into a black puddle as it did earlier when he first revealed his true form. This time, however, he reconstituted into a small, long-horned owl. The spaceman took flight and entered through one of the back gashes left by his brethren.

Inside, the cockpit rocked back and forth as sparks emanated from the walls.

"Kid, Draco can't take much more of this!" Ekchuah exclaimed.

"I'm working on it!"

"Remember, everything has a vital point," Ramona told him calmly. She had hoped that he could take this beast down. Though at this point, faith was all the young assistant could provide. Never, over the course of her life, had she felt as helpless as she did now.

Eric contemplated what weakness a wolf-man would have and remembered they had a sensitive nose, a trait he could greatly take advantage of. Draco Azul's scarf wrapped around the Dogman's neck, holding it in place long enough for the mech to grab onto the wolf's muzzle. Eric gripped onto its snout with as much strength as he could muster. Greenish blood gushed out of the wolf beast's nostrils as it howled in agony. The disturbing sound of crackles signified Draco Azul was slowly breaking his adversary's nose.

The pain was too much, causing the Dogman to release Draco Azul while the man-beast whined in agony as the giant robot held its broken muzzle. With its opponent distracted, Eric had his gargantuan puppet deliver a powerful blow to the abs, its arm blade piercing the wolf's abdomen. The monster coughed up more inhuman fluids before a massive fist came crashing into his face, shattering whatever was left of his mouth.

With such a blow to the head, the creature lost all consciousness as his body slid off his enemy's blades and fell to the streets below. Slowly, the Dogman began to morph anew, becoming less muscular and mangy in the process. The body restructured itself back into a humanoid form while carrying over the severe damage brought on by Earth's guardian.

As it lost its animalistic features, the body shriveled down into what looked like a raisin from the mech's larger than life perspective. What was a towering wolf was now the recognizable figure of the Dogman's unconscious human form. Draco Azul bent down, slowly scooped up the tiny terror, and kept it in its metallic grasp. Eric looked all around for any signs of the owl-men and the Nagual from before. Yet, to his surprise, they were nowhere in sight.

In the cockpit, Eric sighed in relief that he was at least able to finally take down the brute.

"Good job, kid. Now let's go find the others before-" Ekchuah said just as he, Ramona, and Eric caught sight of the remaining owl-men as they rained down from above.

"Damn!" cursed Eric as he attempted once more to swipe at the tornado of avian harpies that encompassed him. "They were flying over us this whole time!"

As the winged terrors continued to damage the surface of Draco Azul's armor, Ekchuah knew that it was only a matter of time before they managed the breach through their mech's hull.

"We gotta get outta here now while we still have the wolf guy."

Hello, a calm voice echoed in the two human's heads.

While Eric continued to fend off the owl-men, Ramona veered to find the Nagual in the cockpit, mere feet from them. Ekchuah quickly noticed right after hearing her gasp.

"What's going on?" a panicked Eric asked.

"It's here," Ramona whispered before her fear enveloped her. "The Nagual's inside!"

He lunged at Ramona, but before he could reach her Ekchuah activated the cockpit's security system with a wave of his arms. Two mechanical appendages armed with tasers unfolded from the walls and aimed towards the alien's ghostly visage. Realizing there was no way to the girl, the vampiric monster avoided the tasers and set his sights on the next best thing.

"Eric!"

"Look out, kid!"

75

The Nagual grabbed Eric by the back of his neck and tore him off his visor with ease. The mech pilot tried to get loose, but the hold was too intense. To make matters worse, Eric could feel the vampire's fingers piercing through his normally indestructible nanosuit and into his blood vessels. He struggled less and less, and he began feeling drained of his energy. The young warrior wondered if this was the Nagual feeding off his blood. Eric knew that if he did not free himself, he would become another slave to the Nagual's disgusting decree, or even worse, dead.

Horrified, Ramona sprinted towards the two of them and attempted to stab the alien's back with her knife. Unfortunately, the futile attempt did nothing to loosen the Nagual's grip as the blade failed to cut deep enough into his skin. In response, the invader twisted his neck and stared intensely down at Ramona. Like before, she began to sense the anger and sorrow in his eyes.

Just as Ekchuah's security arms dived after the vampire, the intruder tossed the young mech pilot aside and morphed into gelatinous goo before slithering into the back room that contained Eric and Ramona's sleeping quarters. There the Nagual revealed the means to his preposterous entrances, a small hole dug from one of the gashes made into Draco Azul's back. As Ramona gave chased the mess of slime shifted once more, this time into the owl form he used to get inside, and soared out of the giant robot, leaving his minions to finish the job.

Ekchuah knew they needed to escape, pronto. On the floor, Eric held onto this neck, screaming from a new burning sensation. Ramona kneeled to check the damage.

"How is he?" questioned an alarmed Ekchuah.

"His heartbeat is going crazy and he's bleeding a lot!"

Realizing his pupil needed medical attention as soon as possible, Ekchuah used his AI programming to activate the mech's autopilot and make a hasty retreat. Outside, the titanic automaton stood in a neutral stance, the Dogman still in its firm grasp. Draco Azul then activated its large jet plane-like wings, causing the ghouls to stare in confusion, baffled at what this strange blue behemoth was going to do.

The roar of the metal titan's rockets went off and all the owl-men flew away as the screeching sound was too much for their ears to bear. No longer swarmed with airborne enemies, the azure warrior leapt into the air and soared across the sky. Once the aggravating noise had ceased, all the Nagual caught sight of was the giant robot's quick disappearance.

Brothers and sisters! They escaped into the sky! Don't let them get away, the Nagual telepathically ordered all his minions.

The beasts each leered at the shrinking figure of Draco Azul, heading for the nearby mountains. All of them screeched at the mech that had moments ago caused them great pain. They ascended to the skies to pursue their prey.

Back in the giant automaton's cockpit, Ramona struggled to carry Eric up to the second room where the Nagual entered from. These four walls would act as the pair's studio apartment where the two would retire every night. Ekchuah meanwhile went right to work patching up the hole in the wall with a temporary sheet of metal using this room's twin mechanical arms, one with a claw and the other with a blowtorch.

"On your feet," Ramona said while she slowly threw her friend's arm over her back, allowing him to lean on her.

Eric screamed out again as he slowly stood. The pilot's companion put her hand over his forehead to feel his temperature where she noted that the mech pilot was burning up with a fever. Slowly, she noticed Eric's skin growing paler right before her eyes. She despised seeing her friend in such pain, but he needed to get to the bed in the shelter room to recover. No way was Ramona going to stand there and watch him wither on the cold metal floor. Slowly, they walked over to the room, stopping a few times when the pain was too much for Eric.

"Easy there," she said.

Smiling warmly, the AI noticed how devoted Ramona was to helping their friend. This moment would not last long as an alarm then went off. Ekchuah opened a holographic screen before him that revealed the worst news for them at a time like this.

Their pursuers had caught up to them, hundreds of owl monsters having tailed the giant robot to the mountain. The AI could not risk fighting with Draco Azul in such terrible shape. In addition, fighting would only increase the pressure on his systems as he was never programmed to control the entire robot beyond moving the giant from one location to another. Doing anything more than that would cause his entire program to shut down permanently. Such a limitation was put in place to ensure that only a human could ever take responsibility for the raw power of the metallic behemoth. For the time being, the only thing Ekchuah could do was stay on course.

The ghouls homed in on their target and increased their speed until they were right above Draco Azul. They dived down and made impact on their prey, causing the cockpit to jostle around. All the animal-like abominations pecked and clawed at its armored plating. Some of the owl-men converted to man-bats similar to the one Eric and Ramona encountered the previous day.

Desperate to cause some level of damage, the beastly figures bit down on the metal armor. They desired nothing but to tear this strange being to pieces and go after the prey that was kept within it. Each ghoul could smell of blood from inside the mech, the aroma of fresh prey to feast on. It was too irresistible to simply ignore that they all caught their scent.

"Ekchuah! Don't just stand there. Do something!" Ramona shouted at the AI.

She was not aware that the AI was incapable of retaliating. Ekchuah heard her demand but didn't have the time to explain. He knew that if he didn't act fast, they would all be in dire trouble.

"They're right on top of us!" she added.

"I know, but I wasn't exactly programmed to fight, okay?"

Ramona was caught by surprise. Was that why Eric always did all the fighting? As confused as she was with the abrupt answer, there was no time to dwell on the thought.

"C'mon! C'mon!" Ekchuah said to himself as he steered the mech towards Copper Canyon, a location he found on his map.

Miraculously, several gorges were up ahead. This caused the AI to further examine the mountains and brainstorm an idea. The flying ghouls would chase them down while they were in the air but he could use the natural structures to lose them and escape.

"Got any ideas on how to lose them?"

"Think I do. Hold on tight!"

Ekchuah moved the mech down into the rocky ravine below. Like sheep, the man-bats and owl-men that weren't already attached to the metal warrior pursued their target. The titan swiftly propelled into the tight crevices of the mountains. Barely large enough for the two-hundred-foot-tall automaton to slip through, the winged monsters that kept digging at the giant's back were crushed to death as their bodies scraped against the rocky terrain of the cliffs. Draco Azul went deeper and deeper, through jagged cliffs and tight crevices. The owl and bat abominations tried to keep up, gradually becoming more confused and overexerted by this new complex area.

It turned out that the only thing the ghouls could do was to split up and catch the robot from multiple paths. This proved to be a large mistake as it only divided their swarm and caused them to lose their way in the unfamiliar terrain.

Ekchuah steadily saw the number of the aerial creatures decrease by the minute until the last of them fell to the ground below out of exhaustion.

The holographic mentor sighed in relief, as he had finally gotten the monsters off their tail for the moment by overwhelming them like rats in a maze. He had dispatched the demons just in the nick of time, as he could feel his systems overheating from Draco Azul's complex controls. The AI slowly piloted the mech to a spot in a neighboring canyon. Finally, the azure titan slowly descended to the ground and softly landed. For now, the three of them were safe and sound.

A while later, the mech opened its chest cavity and dropped the Dogman they captured earlier within its chassis. Ekchuah's mechanical arms dragged the naked ghoul and sat it on the chair Ramona usually sat in. The woman tied him up using the same restraints used during their fights with the Diablos, ensuring their prisoner would not be escaping anytime soon. Once they were finished, Ekchuah and Ramona took a long look at the situation as they both realized the exact same thing. How were they going to stop the Nagual now that Eric, the only means of piloting Draco Azul, was out of commission?

CHAPTER 8

Within the chassis of the mighty robot, the crew found themselves in hot water. Their pilot was out of action, their mech was in deep need of repairs, and their foe's forces were getting stronger. They did not have any means of going on the offence or the defense. What they desperately needed was a game plan.

The resilient AI focused on his two main goals. The first was to manage the repairs to Draco Azul. He had the nanotech working overtime to get the giant fully functional. This proved difficult as the Nagual and his lackeys had dealt an immense level of damage not just to the automaton's armor, but its inner mechanisms as well.

His second aim was to draw a blood sample from the unconscious Dogman, still tied to Ramona's chair after being beaten within an inch of his life by Eric. A needle was injected into the ghoul, slowly pulling out his blood in the hopes to find the secret to the inner workings of the alien vampire. Once the mechanical appendage from the cockpit's walls extracted the sample, the holographic program activated Draco Azul's medical system to further examine the DNA. Ekchuah was careful not to create too much noise, as he did not want to awaken the potentially dangerous Dogman. The last thing they needed was to deal with a ghoul while they were in such a vulnerable state.

The Dogman was indeed still unconscious. The battle with the blue bot took more out of the ghoul than Ekchuah originally thought. Its wounds were still in the process of healing, even though it had been several hours since his fight. Most significant were the injuries to the abdominal organs that had been sliced apart by the mech's blades.

Once Ekchuah got to work analyzing the sample, his eyes widened at the revelation of how the Nagual's virus of sorts worked. The genetic structuring of the ghoul was very complex. The jet-black cells of the alien gradually consumed the last of the normal blood cells of the former human. What was worse was that these foreign cells were expiring as their ineffective mitochondria required an excessive amount of energy. This would explain the ghouls' rabid hunger.

The living program then noticed several cells that didn't appear in the bat-ghoul's blood. They looked very familiar, yet they didn't resemble any of the samples on record from the catalogue of life forms the giant robot encountered on Earth, not even the Nagual's. As soon as Ekchuah brought up a list of Draco Azul's enemies, a match was made absolutely clear. Within the mutated cells of the ghoul was the genetic makeup of the two-headed Diablo. The AI suspected that if the Nagual repeated this process, they were most certainly going to face an army of gargantuan ghoul-Diablo hybrids.

Ekchuah heard gentle footsteps getting close to him, which turned out to be Ramona. She was finally able to calm Eric down and he was resting in the back room.

"How's the kid?" Ekchuah asked his friend and ally.

"He's stable for the moment. I put the restraints on him as you suggested, because... you know."

The hologram nodded, as he knew what she was too hesitant to say. Earlier Ekchuah had run the exact same blood test on his pupil prior to working on the Dogman. To their shock, Eric's body was slowly, but surely, becoming another ghoul. Though his genetic sample had not yet developed the same self-destructing behavior Ekchuah witnessed in the Dogman, meaning his transformation was far from complete. Exactly how long he had until that was to happen was anyone's guess, unfortunately. For the time being, their only option was to keep him restrained.

"Any luck so far?" Ramona asked, trying to change the subject. The woman was hopeful Ekchuah found something in the time she spent comforting her companion. Instead, the AI groaned, a clear indication things were about to go from bad to worse.

"This isn't going to be easy. Just found out the Nagual's infection consumes and changes people on a cellular level, causing an intense need to feed. Those he infected won't last for long without consuming flesh."

Ramona's eyes widened in horror.

"S-so all those people-"

"-are stuck as the Nagual's underlings. If he succeeds at converting everyone into ghouls, the whole human race is as good as gone."

The 27-year-old woman was terrified. Eric and every one of those people were in danger. She tried to think of any other way they could halt the process. Then, a sudden thought occurred. If the Nagual was like the vampiric creatures of legend, then perhaps killing the source could be the solution. The infection might stop all together once he was taken out of the picture.

Ramona also remembered her encounter with the Nagual, physically and mentally observing the alien's desolation and fury. If a creature like him could experience such human emotions, perhaps it was possible to reason with him. The less bloodshed, the better they would be able to save all of those currently under the creature's control.

"What if we captured the Nagual, then get him to tell us how to stop the infection?"

"Hmm," the mentor-figure pondered. "It's not out of the question. Problem is that we have no one to pilot Draco right now, and we'll need one if that plan goes awry. That's not all, though."

"What do you mean?"

"I was looking at our friend's blood here to see how the ghouls function and found something alarming. There are some blood cells that resemble… the last Diablo we fought."

"¡No puede ser!" Ramona gasped in disbelief.

"He must've absorbed the monster's blood into his systems some time before we killed him."

"That explains the cuts we saw on the Diablo in that news report."

"Right. I figured they had a hand in that, but I never realized they were capable of acquiring such power. Now, come look at this."

Ekchuah invited her to look at a holographic monitor displaying the cells he was previously analyzing. There Ramona saw the dead human cells along with two foreign types of genetic material that were violet and black. These two cells were clashing as if trying to consume each other.

"The Diablo cells are fighting against the Nagual's for dominance. It's like a more extreme case of autoimmune disorder. The difference is this is not just the immune system at work, but the invading cells trying to restructure their host. While the overall organism would appear stronger, this struggle for power will leave these creatures unstable and even more dangerous."

Just then, Ramona remembered her companion's condition.

"What about Eric?" she asked.

Ekchuah brought up a second holographic screen showcasing another blood sample.

"Thankfully, Eric's blood has zero traces of these Diablo cells, which means the Nagual hadn't consumed any of the monster's blood by the time he infected him. We should be lucky."

Suddenly a hissing sound echoed through the chamber, followed by loud banging coming from the back room. Ramona rushed over to the room, thinking Eric was in trouble. However, as soon as the thick metallic door opened, the young lady came face to face with her friend... only he barely resembled the man he once was. His pale skin and the green saliva dripping out of his mouth were both signs that the infection had corrupted his body faster than they had previously expected.

Ramona took a few steps away from the transformed young man. Behind him, she could see the broken metal locks that earlier kept him in place. He took two steps towards her like a rabid dog before stopping momentarily. Both Eckhuah and Ramona witnessed Eric's eyes change. The pilot's sclera was still jet black, yet his brown irises and black pupils were back to normal. His fists clenched as he began hitting himself repeatedly. It was clear that Eric was trying desperately to control himself. The man's face displayed great frustration.

"I-I c-can't... stop!"

Making matters worse, the Dogman awoke and shrieked from the commotion. Seething with rage from his humiliating defeat and to the hunger he felt from the fresh human blood that he could smell, the vampiric entity attempted to break free from captivity. With very little time, Eckhuah seized the moment to ensure Ramona's safety. He activated another mechanical arm and manipulated it to grab ahold of his protégé's long coat.

"Hey kid, catch!" shouted the AI as he tossed the garment over to Eric.

The young man instinctively caught it and stared at the brown piece of clothing. Suddenly, tears spilled from his blackened eyes before falling on his wardrobe. He grabbed onto it tightly before mustering enough strength to speak.

"Th-Thanks... c-c-coach. I-I'm heading back in. Lock the d-d-door. Don't let me out, under any c-c-circumstances!" Eric threw the jacket over his shoulders and started walking back into his makeshift bunker.

"Eric, wait!" Ramona wasn't sure why she asked him to stop, despite his condition. Perhaps she wanted to see if her friend was alright, or maybe she just wanted to see his face just one last time.

Once Eric passed the doorway, he turned slightly to face his partner-in-crime. The now pale man mustered a slight smile to hide his pain and winked at her before the doors closed on him. Extra locks could be heard from within the sliding door's mechanics, indicating Ekchuah was already hard at work to reinforce the security separating them from their companion.

Tears streamed down the woman's face. Never before had she seen her friend in such a tragic state, and there was nothing she could do to help with his pain. Their only chance now was to find a cure. To do that, they needed to unlock the secrets to what made their captive foe tick. Her attention was drawn back to the Dogman, who had fallen unconscious once more. He had clearly tired himself out when he tried to break free. The pair were thankful that the ghoul had yet to fully regain his strength.

With both immediate threats subsided, Ramona remembered the significance of Eric's coat.

"How did you know he'd react that way?" she asked her only friend left to console her.

"Oh, that? Well, there's a whole story behind that coat he always carries."

"What happened?"

"Well, I suppose Eric would've told you sooner or later. Just before we met you, Eric took a short vacation to Ensenada up in Baja California. He needed some time away from the constant training and I thought it would do him some good.

"Unfortunately, a Diablo followed us there and started doing what every one of those miserable creatures do. Eric beat it, of course, but in the process, he lost several people he befriended during his stay, the Rodriguez family. The father had apparently given him his coat right before Eric had to let them go and fight the Diablo. Unfortunately, they were... caught in the crossfire. The kid still blames himself for their deaths, thinking he brought the monster to Ensenada. To this day he wears that coat in their memory."

Upon hearing the hologram regale his tale, everything clicked for Ramona. Eric's reluctance to share the purpose behind his long coat, as well as his overprotective nature whenever she volunteered to put herself in harm's way. He never wanted to lose anyone the same way he lost the Rodriguez family again.

"Touching story. I guess you humans really do value life after all."

A chill ran down Ramona's spine as she heard the Dogman suddenly speaking. On top of the fact that he was suddenly using fluent English, his demeanor was no longer that of the rabid monster that once tried to break free of his shackles. Now, he was calm, collected, and carried a smug aura about him.

"Unfortunately, it doesn't excuse the centuries of oppression you have placed on my people. All the death. All the torture. It's far too late to reconcile with the actions you have made!"

"What are you going on about?" asked the puzzled AI. "You were a human once. How would you know what the Naguals have been through? If I knew any better, I'd say you thought you actually were one."

"That's because he is," stated Ramona, who recognized the tone in the Dogman's voice. It was the same consciousness that was shared between him and the alien. "You're the Nagual, aren't you? You're using this body like a puppet."

"Clever girl. I was right to share my innermost thoughts with you," the Dogman curled his lips to reveal a grizzly smile, one that was anything but pleasant. "I placed an enormous amount of mental control over this particular subject to the point where he can act as an extension of my own will remotely, while all this time I hid in plain sight."

"Do you control all your lackeys like this?" the AI asked as he continued the interrogation.

"How dare you address my family as such!" the Nagual's avatar shouted at the hologram. "They are no 'lackeys,' as you call them." The puppet then turned his attention back towards the young lady. "Each one of my relatives are as precious to me as any of yours, Ramona."

"How do you know my name?" demanded the woman, caught off guard by the alien's knowledge.

"Oh, I know all about you from the moment I laid my eyes on you. It was rather curious as to how someone with such disdain for those wretched dog fights would ever be caught attending one. Unless, however, there were ulterior motives at hand. So, when I allowed you to peer into my mind, I did the same to you. I learned of both Eric and Draco Azul. Everything I needed to bypass your defenses and nullify your greatest asset!"

Ramona was disgusted. This monster had dared to invade her innermost thoughts and used her life for his sick, twisted games. She remembered the feeling of melancholy from the Nagual the first time Ramona gazed into his eyes. The young woman recalled that vision of another world and other beings like him. Was any of it real or was it all some fantasy made to distract her to allow the being to peer into her very soul?

"Then explain that vision from before. Was that your home? Your people?"

"Indeed, they were." The proxy looked down at the floor before he started whimpering.

Ramona wondered if she had struck an emotional nerve.

"Our home has long been lost to time. We never caused anyone harm, we only meant to live and thrive on our own soil. Perhaps it was the universe's aberrant cruelty, as everything and everyone slowly perished as our sun expanded. Our world was incinerated with every solar flare, and I was forced to watch our entire legacy burn to ash, then see those very ashes vaporize.

"Before things worsened, I spent decades trying to find a means for our kind to escape. I eventually developed a way of enhancing our natural shape-shifting ability to survive on other planets. Soon afterwards, our spacecrafts abandoned what was once our home and floated for ages in the frigidness of the black, starry void. My ship lost communication with the others as we were forced to go our separate ways, thus increasing our species' chances of finding a suitable planet. I don't know if the others are still out there, though I believe some of them are.

"My family spent what must have felt like a millennia roaming the stars before we found Earth. There, we sought out one thing-"

"Conquest?" queried Ekchuah.

"No…" The Nagual-controlled Dogman closed his eyes. "Comfort."

Both Ramona and Eckhuah were taken aback by the refugee's goal.

"We had no idea what to expect. We walked into a world where the lifeforms wore simple garbs, developed farming, cultivated a simple civilization, and worshiped deities. If you humans were anything like my kind, then there was a glimmer of hope we could be assisted. To be given refuge and be greeted as brothers… alas, we were not. Quickly, we learned what humans were truly like."

Ramona understood that during that time, no one would have understood the displaced Naguals. The natives would have seen them as monsters and judged as nothing but such.

"That's not how we-"

"They all viewed us as anomalies! Gave us a name to be frightened of! Depicted me and my people as demons! That continued for century after century as my kind was hunted. Now I am the last of my kind, doomed to spend a lifetime stuck on this feeble mudball of a planet. However, hope came in the form of what you call the 'Diablos.' It was then I decided I was going to ensure that my kind would rise up. So, here I am."

Ramona and Ekchuah were floored by the Nagual's odyssey. The leather-clad woman in particular felt a wave of empathy wash over her. His motivations made everything clear to them. A thought materialized that perhaps if he really scanned all her memories when the two of them mind melded, perhaps he also saw the good that she and her friends have done.

"Let me ask you this. You saw everything. Eric, Eckhuah, and Draco Azul. But did you truly see everything? My life, friends, family, even the good people I've met."

The Nagual-Dogman intentionally ignored her. Ramona knew then that he must have seen those visions.

"I'm sorry you came here at the wrong time," Ramona attempted to explain. "But times have changed. Humanity has changed. We've learned to embrace peace."

"Has it though? I've seen throughout the decades how the ones with power handle 'peace' with others of your kind."

"There will always be idiots out there, but they don't make up most of us."

"You're right, they make up all of you. And once I have achieved my goal, there will soon be none of you!"

The Dogman mustered all his strength and at long last freed himself from his metal bonds. He transformed one last time into his beastly canine form with much quicker results.

"Given your unique memories," the wolf-like creature howled as it slobbered green spit all over the floor, "I thought you deserved an explanation as to the fate of your race before I eliminate you murderers once and for all!"

The monster sprung towards a panicked Ramona. Seeing this attack coming from a mile away, the AI unleashed Draco Azul's security system. Four mechanical arms aimed their taser-like devices at the Dogman from all corners. Wailing in excruciating pain, the ghoul watched helplessly as the hologram turned up the voltage ever so higher. The beast's skin seared from the intense jolts that struck his body.

After a good minute of electrocution, Eckhuah turned off the system once the enemy's howls went quiet. The Dogman fell limp to the floor. His limbs twitched, displaying what little amount of life he had. Slowly his spasms lessened by the second before ultimately coming to a complete stop.

CHAPTER 9

Throughout the next day, the beautiful city of Chihuahua was in a state of dystopian purgatory. After the showdown between Draco Azul and the giant wolf-man, a battle so destructive that it caught the attention of the government within hours, an evacuation of the citizens of Durango state was hastily executed. The rushed and poorly planned migration yielded incomplete results, with only seventy percent of the populace successfully taken out of most major cities. Hoping help would come soon, the remainder had zero means of leaving the cities whether it was due to a lack of funds, transportation, or were incapable of leaving behind loved ones unable to travel themselves. For the time being, these civilians were forced to depend on the experienced soldiers of the Mexican military to protect them.

The government's best men were of no importance to the Nagual, however, as he had already set his sights on one city, Chihuahua, the location that started it all. Following the raid on the Diablo encampment, the alien had left several of his minions in Chihuahua to slowly gather their strength discreetly through the murders of several more victims. Recently, however, the ghouls' tactics pre-programmed into their brains by the Nagual began to change. As they grew stronger, they preferred tearing their targets to pieces for the rich nutrition they craved, leaving behind greater messes in the process.

Ghouls ran rampant through the streets, hunting soldiers and innocent residents alike for their vital fluid. It was a nightmare that only the most heartless souls could devise. Many hoped that the great azure mech, Draco Azul, would arrive at their city once more and take care of these monsters. Alas, their guardian was nowhere in sight.

Within the pandemonium, a 35-year-old man named Miguel watched the commotion outside from his boarded-up first-floor apartment. Inside the household, his eight-year-old daughter, Verónica, was close behind him, petrified over the deafening cries of the community. The father monitored the scenario through the cracks in the wooden barricade. Outside, he found images he could never let his little girl bear witness to, as the horror would scar her for the rest of her life. The man was already forced to gaze upon the image of a woman's body devoured by devils that were once members of their peaceful neighborhood.

He yearned to save the love of his life, whose current whereabouts were unknown. Yet, it was a failed exercise in thought as any hope of saving his wife outside was as dead as the woman's lifeless corpse. Miguel knew he and his daughter had to escape if they wanted to avoid that victim's fate.

"Mommy is going to be okay, right?" the innocent child asked.

The man never told her about his wife's grim fate. He and his spouse were out for a night as part of their neighborhood watch in the wake of multiple missing person reports, unaware of the true danger that plagued their city. While they were out, their neighbor offered to babysit their child. An hour into their walk, an emergency announcement stemmed from the sudden incursion of the ghouls. The duo promptly rushed home, anxious about the safety of their child.

On the journey back to their apartment building, the two were stopped by a pair of soldiers in the middle of the road. Strangely, neither of them had weapons in their hands. Miguel shined his flashlight at them, revealing their torn uniforms and fatigued expressions on their faces, like they had been to Hell and back. One serviceman veered towards the pair with a grim expression and glowing eyes. Miguel quickly realized that the creatures he was looking at were no longer men. They were the monsters they had heard about on the news, during the emergency broadcast. The very ones that had been attacking and mutilating everyone in sight.

In a daring move, the mother threw her flashlight at the figure and ran. She led the zombie-like men away from the apartment so her husband could get to their daughter. The rattled man refused to leave her behind, but her final words convinced him otherwise. To her, he would be more than capable of keeping their daughter alive. As much as he feared for his love's fate, he kept the illusion that she was alive to give his daughter, and himself, a glimmer of conviction.

"She'll be fine. She's hiding like we are, but in another building."

"Daddy, why is everyone hurting each other?"

Verónica began to weep. Tears slowly rolled down her face. No one knew why all of this was happening. When he returned to the apartment complex, completely shaken to his very core, he found his daughter hidden in their closet with their neighbor guarding the door. As they left to check on everyone else, Miguel held his dear child, the only precious thing he had left.

"I don't know, sweety. I just don't know. But we'll get out of this."

After the two embraced, the man grinned weakly at his daughter. He wiped the tears off her face. This touching moment did not last long though, as several pairs of clawed hands broke through the bordered-up walls and windows. These demons could pick up the scent of fresh blood. The hellspawns' sense of smell was so keen that they could recognize how old their prey was on scent alone. Prior to breaking in, they had already visualized their quarry as an adult and child upon detecting their potential meal.

Terrified, Miguel picked up his daughter and sought the nearest exit. He explored what few exits remained in their cramped apartment. The desperate father quickly found that there was no escape from their home as all the exits were filled with the pale flailing limbs of the monsters.

Past his prime, the father no longer possessed the strength he once had in his younger days. Miguel knew that a physical confrontation with the creatures would spell certain death for both he and his daughter. Just then, a light bulb went off in his head. He remembered the door in his building that led to an alley where his daughter would play.

The man took his child and dashed into the hallway towards the back. Once he exited his home, he found ghouls crowding the pathway, each of them marching slowly towards them. He also noticed a narrow pathway to his left and immediately took it.

Miguel sprinted as fast as he could to his car parked several blocks away. He saw others with the same idea achieve varying results. Some vehicles looked abandoned while others were totaled and bloodied. The man looked behind him to see if they were still being pursued. The ghouls all shoved themselves through the pathway as they persisted to chase down the small family.

At last, he and his daughter made it to their car, a worn-out SUV. The vehicle appeared to have sustained some superficial damage as a result of the ghouls' attack, but it was still clearly operational. Hastily placing his daughter in the back seat, the father then jumped into the driver's seat. He breathlessly tried to ignite the engine. Unfortunately, it would not start as the ghouls were quickly closing in on them.

"Goddammit! Start already!" Miguel screamed, banging on the dashboard.

It appeared his van would not come to life at the worst possible time. This was the first time his daughter observed any sign of vulnerability from the sole guardian she had left.

It frightened the young girl. Her father always knew how to make things better. Mercifully, after four attempts, the motor roared to life.

Miguel floored the gas pedal into high gear. The SUV's wheels spun at a hasty pace. What was left of the small family accelerated forth, with the image of the revenants gradually shrinking. The man sighed, relieved they had gotten away. His daughter peeked through the window, curious about all the commotion. The first thing she saw was a boy, no older than she was, getting mauled by two beasts, one bird-like and the other a werewolf.

That was all the girl needed to see before she ducked down into her chair, pulled her knees up to her chest, and buried her head. Her father paid no attention, as he needed to ensure their survival and was doing his best to stay focused on that goal. In a flash, one of the monsters sprung onto the windshield of the car. Before Miguel could make out the silhouette of the attacker, the windshield was already smashed, leaving a spiderweb of cracks.

As visibility was next to impossible, he swerved in different directions trying to throw the beast off. In spite of the lack of a clear field of view, he could still make out that the ghoul was stubbornly clinging to the front of his car. The creature wasn't going to release its clutches willingly.

At last, the ghoul leaped off the vehicle, improving Miguel's field of view through the broken windshield. Ahead of him was a looming stockpile of demolished automobiles. From the shattered windshields on several of the cars, he guessed that other people trying to flee the carnage in the city were attacked in the same manner as he had just been. The result was that the drivers slammed into each other, causing a pile up that only made them easier prey for the ghouls that were attacking them.

In a failed attempt to avoid the bulk of the destroyed vehicles, he steered the car hard to the right. While his actions allowed him to avoid slamming directly into the mountainous wreck, he still hit the side of the piled automobiles. Instinctively, the father reached out to his little girl and shielded her mere moments before impact. Miguel covered his daughter's eyes with his forearm and squinted his own. While his actions prevented the shattered glass from piercing their eyes, the rest of their bodies were still unprotected. A maelstrom of shards from the broken windshield sliced into their exposed flesh. Through his hand, the man heard his daughter's muffled scream of fear and pain.

As Miguel opened his eyes, he recognized the situation he and Verónica were in. From a distance, he heard the monsters closing in on the two of them. With all his senses heightened, the man could feel the adrenaline coursing through his body. He could hear their footsteps, one after another. Miguel was quick to unfasten his and his daughter's seat belts, ignoring the excruciating pain brought on by the impaled glass. He stepped out of the vehicle very carefully, getting his bearings as he removed the glass from his limbs before holding Verónica tightly in his arms. She was the most precious thing to him and no matter the consequences, he was not going to let her die at the hands of some mindless, drool-ridden walking corpses.

As soon as he started moving away from the car, he heard the sound of metal creaking. Something had jumped onto the crashed junk heap. What he witnessed was too shocking for him to describe. His worst fears had come to life.

"*What's wrong with mommy?*" the child asked.

Her dad did not respond to her innocent question for he was still processing the sight of the pale form that was once his wife. Verónica couldn't understand what had become of the person who had given her life. The figure she recognized as her mother stared at them while her salivating mouth uttered a low, guttural sound.

Miguel took a few steps back before sprinting as fast as he could. He endured every ounce of pain his punctured body felt, but this was unfortunately not enough to escape his fate. His wife pounced on him, forcing him face first into the pavement. Without a second thought, the man released his daughter from his tight grip and pushed her away from the two of them.

The possessed mother grabbed onto his neck and began sucking his essence. He could feel his body convulse and twitch. On top of that, he heard more of the demons gathering around them.

"*G-go!*" Miguel screamed out to his daughter.

He turned back to his former lover and used the last of his strength to strangle her neck. This was just to distract her from attacking their daughter. Unfortunately, their little girl did not move an inch.

"*Daddy, what's happening?*" she cried out, her face riddled in tears.

The girl was too young to understand the weight of what was taking place. Why were her parents fighting? Why did her mother look different? Why were people dying? Verónica looked to her parental figures for guidance in a vain attempt to make any sense of her crumbling world.

The thing that was once her mother reacted to her little girl's pleads with an unnatural emerald gaze. She hissed at her daughter and slobbered green mucus. Her husband attempted to pull her closer while his crimson fluids poured down from his neck. He felt weaker by the second, but as long as his heart kept beating he would keep his child safe.

"*I'm gonna help your mother! Just run and don't look back!*"

Like any well-behaved child, Verónica ran as fast as her little legs could carry her. She dared not give a second glance even though she wanted to turn back and help her parents in any way she could.

"*Aaaaagh!*" the father yelled out as he was maimed.

His daughter heard the resonate of cracked bones. She had no idea what to do or where to go. All she could do was rush down the streets of her hometown. The young girl's heart was beating faster than an Olympic sprinter during a marathon. Adrenaline filled her young body enough to push herself past her normal limits.

As the child ran aimlessly, she thought about all her friends and where they might be. She wondered if they could be in the same situation as she was in. Or worse, if they had they been turned into monsters like her mother.

Verónica was deluged with a level of anxiety that no child should experience. Through her blurred vision she saw a humanoid outline that she closed in on. The figure was the only being that didn't look like the other malicious fiends.

"Mister! Mister! Please, help me! My mommy and daddy are in trouble!"

She got on her knees and pleaded to the stranger. It was then that she finally got a good look at the man. His appearance was startling. The stranger's body was very thin and uncanny with skin paler than an apparition. His eyes glared down at her with an expression that was somehow both welcoming and chilling. He lowered himself to one knee and patted the girl's head.

No need to worry, little one. Your father is going to join your mother and become more than what he is currently. And soon, you'll be joining them as well.

The stranger exposited to her in a calm and buoyant manner. She tilted her head, confused by the strange words. Verónica was unable to figure out how she could even hear his words when he had no mouth. What the child failed to comprehend was that this was the ghoul's leader, the Nagual. After gaining more recruits in the hills of Ojuela, he decided to return to the city where it all began to regroup with his forces. Within a matter of hours, the Nagual had led his newly created followers across the city as he prepared to purge the world of the human race.

For the moment, the vampire's words were just a distraction. His minions grabbed the small human by the ankles and swept her off the ground. The Nagual could not have been more gratified than to welcome such an innocent soul into his family.

That was until his kin did something unexpected. They savagely ripped the wailing girl apart, tossing pieces of her aside like garbage. To the best of the alien's knowledge, this contrasted with how the beasts usually fed. The callousness of it abhorred him.

Humans were supposed to be slaughtered by draining them of their blood, not tearing them to shreds like mindless monsters. He looked back at the father, confirming his similar fate. A gory pile of bones was all that remained of the man.

Stop! We're supposed to only draw their fluids, not slaughter them like animals!

The Nagual shouted at his minions as he pushed them off the girl. He was too late, for the child was already deceased. The ghouls began to contradict their usual behavior as they showed signs of defiance. They pushed their leader out of the pile of guts and meat in a scramble to feed on the remains. This caused the Nagual to be taken aback, aghast at what just ensued.

They're getting worse. Their minds are deteriorating, the alien thought to himself.

He panicked at what could have caused this change, for his subordinates always had a one-track mind, but these were the actions of primitives. The strange being thought back to the Mayans he and his race contended with centuries ago. He tried to deduce if there was any event that could have caused this change in temperament. At first, he figured they were paranoid after they all faced Draco Azul earlier. Perhaps they were more on edge and scared.

Yet, none of them demanded the mech's whereabouts nor sought revenge on the giant. Then, it hit the Nagual like a sack of bricks. All of this started after he made them taste the blood of the Diablo.

Damn Diablo! the Nagual cursed to himself. *No. I underestimated how potent it would be on them. I should have tested its lasting effects thoroughly.*

He then cursed himself even further. Before, they would listen to his every word. Since then, the giant's blood must have affected his family slowly over time as they passed their infection on to new ghouls. While it enhanced their strength, it must be poisonous to their weaker immune systems and distressed their minds in the process.

Brothers and sisters, you must cease this bloodshed! Crave as you see fit, but as Naguals, we mustn't act like the violent primates!

The Nagual tried to catch his followers' attention. Yet, their focus was solely on the ensanguined meal before them. His reactions and dialect were all but an empty cacophony to them. The vampire was left confused and powerless, unable to quell their bloodlust. He gave up and took a stroll around the neighborhood, hoping he could clear his mind and think of a plan.

Poisoning his family was the worst thing he could have done. During his walk he encountered more limbs, heads, and heinous amounts of gore scattered about. The fact that they were human remains didn't bother him. Rather, it was the very thought that his own kind were behind such gruesome acts was what made it harrowing, and he struggled to clear his thoughts until he found a large shadow looming over him.

It was the empowering structure of the Cathedral of Chihuahua. The tannish-colored structure was an intimate icon to the Nagual. The sight of such massive churches always took his nonexistent breath away.

There was something extremely grandiose and dynamic about such architectures. He had heard and seen anecdotes of human families that would visit these locations in search of guidance and miracles from their god. The Nagual's people didn't have a deity they worshipped. That said, his people once believed in a religion that revolved around nontheism.

Perhaps I need more than just my words to guide them.

He walked inside the church to seek a more enlightened way to convince his family to stay on what he believed was the right path. He was not one to pray, but if it helped his family, then he would dive headfirst into this unfamiliar world. The lifeless building's interior was nothing short of exquisite. It was a humongous area, with one path leading to a statue and between it were rows of seats for all to worship within the house of a messiah.

The sight would have been a painting come to life in the eyes of the extraterrestrial had it not been for the rotting remains. However, for the Nagual, he would have to contend with the gruesome decor. He sauntered towards the front and basked in the majesty of the statue before him. The Nagual dropped to his knees and uttered a prayer:

Lords of this world. Me and my people are not your followers, but we've heard of your performance of miracles beyond comprehension. I do not know if you require an offering, but if so, I give you my whole being. My flesh and blood are yours for the taking if need be.

I ask only for one simple request. Please help me. Everyone I love is slowly losing their minds! Please, make them see the light! I know you must despise your creations for the sins they've committed to this world and to my family. I only wish to deliver rightful punishment. I've lost so many... I don't want to lose any more.

CHAPTER 10

Ekchuah and Ramona stood by and watched the madness erupting madness in Chihuahua right before their eyes. The monitors within Draco Azul's cockpit televised the news of the Nagual beginning to spread his vampiric plague across the city. Various sources were soon covering the outbreak of ghouls throughout the country. Within Mexico, cities such as Durango, Monterrey, and Mazatlán all underwent emergency lockdowns. Reports cited that by the end of the week the creatures would take hold of larger cities such as Guadalajara and Mexico City. Meanwhile, the federal government made a worldwide announcement of their continued efforts of evacuations.

At the same time, officials attempted to downplay the situation to keep their citizens from creating further panic. Yet, for all their efforts to quell their ever-increasing fear, all they managed to accomplish was adding more fuel to the fire. Ramona asked Ekchuah to turn off the monitors, having seen enough of the carnage.

"I am not going to sit here and watch everything burn! There has to be something we can do!" Ramona loudly exclaimed.

As she spoke, the sounds of screams and banging erupted from the back door of the cockpit. It was their friend, Eric. After the Nagual successfully infected him with the same toxins that turned his other victims into zombie-like creatures, the young man proved to be in no condition to control the mech. Every several minutes he would strike at the layers of metal that kept him imprisoned as he struggled with the intense pain of becoming another ghoul.

Ekchuah, trying his best not to let his pupil's suffering distract him, had thought long and hard about the right course of action. With Eric out of the picture and the AI's inability to manipulate Draco Azul for long periods of time, there was only one other person who could.

"Well, I do have an idea, but it's risky." The hologram paused. "Very risky."

"Whatever it is, I'll help any way I can!"

The AI grinned hopefully at the girl's determination. Ekchuah admired her headstrong attitude, but he knew just how dangerous this undertaking would be. He would rather not put anyone else through such a traumatic experience, but there were no other options.

"Here's the thing. Neither me nor Eric can pilot the big guy, but you can."

"M-me?" Ekchuah nodded to Ramona.

The young woman was caught off guard by the AI's suggestion.

"Draco Azul's repairs are nearly complete, and right now we need a pilot who can get the job done until we can cure Eric."

"Are you sure? I mean, yeah, I'm willing to do it, but do you think I'm ready?"

Ramona was vastly doubtful of the Ekchuah's proposal. For as long as the young woman had lived, she had witnessed all kinds of physical altercations. Yet, fighting monsters was on a whole other level. One that she could not begin to imagine what it would be like, even after watching Eric fight from the sidelines. The physical and mental toll controlling Draco Azul took on him was enough to tell her it was no enviable task.

"Can't one hundred percent say, but Eric wasn't exactly a pro at this when we started. At first, he was pretty green, but he got the hang of it quicker than I expected. You should be able to get a handle on things with your skills."

Ramona took his words under serious consideration. The AI had mentored every one of Draco Azul's users across countless generations. If he trusted her ability enough, then perhaps he was right. Nevertheless, she still questioned her worthiness in wielding such an immense responsibility. The woman was not certain if she was strong enough to handle the pressure or even skilled enough to beat the Nagual.

"D-do it," a voice said from the other room.

Both Ramona and Ekchuah turned to the source of the audible message. As Ekchuah activated a switch to the controls, one of the holographic monitors turned on. There, the image of the young man stood by the locked sliding door. Eric was significantly paler than usual. His body was covered in sweat and his knuckles were bruised and bloodied from wailing on the walls. For the moment, he managed to keep his newfound feral nature at ease.

Ramona did not look at the monitor as she approached the door, however. She reached out her hand.

"Eric?" her soft voice answered.

Hearing her so close, yet out of his reach, Eric too placed his hand on the barrier that separated them.

"Everyone is counting on you," her friend responded.

These words cut deep into Ramona. She could not doubt herself, as an innumerable amount of lives were now in her hands. If she did not act then and there, the whole world would be in great peril. No matter the risks, this was her chance to change the tide. With newfound determination and fierceness, Ramona muttered three words to Ekchuah.

"I'll do it."

The AI smiled at her answer, pleased that Eric convinced her to do the right thing. Ekchuah also knew he had just as great of a burden ahead of him. He had to train her correctly as he had done with Eric, but in a drastically short amount of time. The AI preferred to give his protégés the full experience and allow them to comprehend Draco Azul's immense power and various abilities. With no time to spare, Ekchuah would have to provide Ramona a crash course in order to ensure her stamina would be built up enough to destroy the Nagual before passing out.

"Be careful," Eric requested.

Ramona drew a confident smirk on her face

"It'll be a cinch," Ramona replied with great assurance.

Through the monitor, the AI could see the young man smile faintly, having heard his friend repeat the same phrase he used to instill confidence in his companion. Suddenly, Eric flinched and groaned. It was agonizing for both of his friends. With much of his energy gone, he slumped against the door and faded into unconsciousness. The physical and mental battle was too great for the young warrior, courtesy of the Nagual.

Ramona felt horrible, as she couldn't imagine how much her friend must be fighting against the vampire's all-consuming influence. She promised herself that the vampire would suffer.

"Let's get started," Ekchuah said as he prepared the cockpit for training.

***

"Mr. Martinez?" a voice called out.

Eric's eyes slowly opened. He found himself in a setting that was very familiar, yet incredibly foreign at the same time. He faced over two dozen students in a small, cramped classroom. These teenage pupils waited for him to continue teaching whatever new history lesson he was supposed to guide them through that day. Prior to taking up the mantle of the Primal Warrior's latest conductor, Eric Martinez was a high school social studies teacher. The young man's mind raced in several directions.

If he is all better, he should be stopping the Nagual with Ramona and Ekchuah. This had to be a dream. It was the only scenario that made sense.

"We're waiting," one student arrogantly said to Eric.

The instructor stood before all of them like a deer in headlights, with no clue where to even begin. For a moment,

106

he rolled with it so as not to embarrass himself. Now that he got a good look at the class, Eric recognized a few of his old students. The pilot theorized that he was reliving a moment when he taught a class of freshmen about World War II before he became enwrapped with Ekchuah and Draco Azul. It was earlier in the school year, with Spring Break right around the corner when the weather began to get hotter and drier.

His students began snickering and jeering at his social awkwardness the longer he stood in silence before them. Some of the class clowns decided it was more fun to throw paper planes at their unmoving target. As Eric was processing where he was, he began to remember exactly why he chose to use his vacation days to start his Spring Break much earlier.

"Umm yes, class. Turn to page…" Eric then shifted through his textbook to find where today's course was supposed to begin. "One ninety-five. For the next three classes, we'll be going over everything about World War II."

Without hesitation, Eric began his lecture, having found himself getting back into the swing of things. The teacher regaled his class about the aftermath of the previous World War as he was writing out the timeline of events on a whiteboard while half of them turned their textbooks to the page and wrote down notes. Everyone else was chatting amongst themselves in a not so discreet manner.

The educator started to come to the grips with the possibility that this may be more than a hallucination and that this scenario could very likely be real. It would certainly put his mind at ease if he knew that the world was not under the threat of any giant monsters or ancient vampires, but then that would also mean his friends, possibly the only ones that he had, were never real to begin with.

One student raised her hand. "I have a question, Mr. Martinez."

"Yes?"

"Do you think history ever got anything wrong?"

Eric did a double take at the query. Never did any of his students ever ask such a question, nor were they the kind to even care about the accuracy of their education. He always had a hard enough time getting his classes invested in their studies in the first place. As suspicious as he was, Eric decided to play along for the moment.

"Well, it's common for there to be misinterpretations of ancient texts or biased reports. Luckily, this point in time is a relatively recent event-"

"-because the stories told here are all lies. You were brainwashed into buying humanity's accomplishments. Making yourselves out to be pioneers and heroes. Lies. All lies!"

The teenager's voice changed as she continued, sounding seamlessly like the Nagual he and Ramona encountered in Ojuela. Just then, all the students' appearances changed one after the other. Their eyes glowed green and spiraling symbols appeared around their faces. Instinctively, Eric tried to summon Draco Azul, only to find that there was no communicator on his wrist.

Left with no other option, the man grabbed one of the wooden meter sticks he had on his desk and broke it in half on his knee. The pilot now had makeshift weapons to use against the ghouls that approached him. Beneath his feet, the floor shook and cracks broke out across the surface. Without warning, the entire lecture room around him collapsed and left Eric falling endlessly in a surreal green and blue void. The young warrior soon ceased descending and was then floating in a barren and empty space.

"None of these choices you made were of your own," said the Nagual's voice, now being heard from all directions. "From being a teacher of warped facts, to being drafted into piloting that machine which takes its toll on its user like a worn battery. But Eric, you can change all of that. Finally, you could be your own man, free to make your own decisions again. You just have to do one thing."

A pair of giant eyes opened in the empty void before Eric. He had endured those ghastly orbs before. They belonged to none other than the Nagual. The young man detected nothing from the intense gaze was but pure, blind fury. It was the same cold glare as when the Nagual intruded inside Draco Azul during their last confrontation.

"Let me in."

Eric felt immense pressure weighing down his entire body. He looked down at his suddenly cold hands. They turned as pale as the alien's face. His nails extended and sharpened as they grew. As he changed, flashes of visions sporadically entered his mind.

He found a future where the Nagual reigned over a ruined world. Cities had crumbled and the ghouls ran rampant. Draco Azul was reduced to a scrap pile scattered across different parts of Mexico with the Nagual using the head as a makeshift castle. Inside the devastated husk of the mech's cranium was the invader sitting upon a thrown made of scrap metal. Beside him were Eric and Ramona, or what was left of them, rendered as the alien's new loyal lapdogs.

Eric yelled out in anguish as he fought to purge himself of these nightmares. He began thinking of all the good people he had known, Ekchuah, Ramona, and especially the Rodriquez family he befriended during the Baja California incident.

"Let me in."

The spiraling void Eric was trapped in changed its gravity. He plummeted further downward, leaving the bluish green void into an endless pitch black pitfall where no light could reach.

"Aaagh!"

Eric could feel his body stretch, becoming twisted and contorted as he fell into this second dark abyss. All the 26-

year-old could do was scream and try his best to still conquer the influence the Nagual had over him.

Like something out of a horror film, Eric woke up in a cold sweat. He investigated his surroundings and found himself in a new location. The ground was soft and muddy. Above him were trees and plants that were greener than any forest he had ever seen. Eric got his bearings and walked through this new world the Nagual threw him into.

"Where are we now?" Eric called out to his captor, infuriated by the mind games he was playing against him.

"Where the lies began," was the entity's reply.

From behind, eight beings were careening towards Eric. Greatly resembling the Nagual, there were some slight differences in armor and skin color. The texture of their epidermis was more vibrant and lively compared to their descendant's pale and pastel appearance. They ran right through Eric as if he wasn't there. They were all breathing heavily, indicating they had been sprinting for a long period of time.

Close behind them were a group of Mesoamerican people who wore pelts of jaguar fur and helmets topped with feathers. Holding shields, spears, and macuahuitls, they charged towards the Nagual's race. They all phased past Eric just as their prey had moments ago. These warriors were the ancient Maya that prospered within Mexico hundreds of years ago. This is where it all began for the Nagual. The very same being finally materialized before Eric. Both acted as spectators to the history that unfolded before them.

"Beneath all of your feet is the blood of my family," said the angered creature. His voice was still spoken out loud within this dream world. "The ones you all slaughtered without a second thought! Now, feast your eyes on my accursed suffering. What plays in my head countless times, like a broken record."

The Maya who led the hunt launched his spear towards the vampires while the rest of his men followed his actions.

Though the Naguals did their best to outrun them, four of the ghouls ended up impaled by the wooden lances. Green blood trickled down the pole and the poor creatures whimpered while attempting to pull out the javelins. In the meantime, the Maya warriors seized their opportunity by using their blades to decapitate the fallen family members.

The indigenous men heard something rustling in the bushes. Armed to the teeth for their prey they waited for whatever it was to reveal itself. Instead of the vampires they sought, five fellow legionaries marched into view, each one holding a member of the Nagual's race. All four of the space visitors were beaten to a bloody pulp.

Eric awoke and was finally back in the studio room where he was locked up.

Tragedy can make or break anyone, lectured the telepathic voice of his enemy. *You'll never understand how it feels to carry on after losing everything you loved. Humans never learn from their mistakes, never allowing reality to sink in.*

"To the contrary," Eric spoke out loud to the voice in his head. "If anyone's got anything to learn, it's you. We humans can learn from our mistakes. That's a lesson you'll learn soon enough when Ramona takes you and all your puppets down."

CHAPTER 11

It was late afternoon as the Sun shone over the still form of Draco Azul, hiding inside its canyon sanctuary. Within the center of the cockpit, Ramona stood still in place. The floor beneath her feet illuminated with a bright white glow.

"How does this work again?" she asked her new mentor.

"Just give it a few seconds," replied Ekchuah. "But before you do that, you might want to remove your jacket. The suit is skintight, but you'll be fine in those clothes."

Ramona had changed outfits, forgoing her normal street wear and instead outfitting herself with the gym clothes she previously used for her sparring session with Eric.

Soon afterwards, millions of nanomachines seeped through the glowing panels of the metal floor and crawled their way up the rookie pilot's legs. To human eyes, the nanomachines had the appearance of blue metallic liquid covering every inch of her body.

"This feels weird," exclaimed Ramona.

"You'll get used to it. Just don't make any sudden movements. The suit needs to calibrate itself for every new user."

As the nanomachines bonded to her body, the semblance of Eric's pilot suit began to take shape. The tech wrapped itself around every square inch of the young lady's body, from her stomach and torso to her individual fingers. The metal suit stopped right at the base of her neck, and the young woman looked down at her new means of manipulating the technological giant. She raised her arms and examined her uniform.

At first, it was a little tight for her liking, yet as she stretched her body, she began to feel more flexible as the suit adjusted to her movements. It was as if it was another layer of skin. She started wondering if Eric felt similarly when he first donned the sapphire uniform.

Then she heard a sound from above and noticed multiple mechanical appendages lowering from the roof. Each one was carrying the rest of her outfit.

"Raise your arms to the side and let the machines do the rest," instructed Ekchuah.

Once Ramona stood in a T-shaped position, the metal limbs positioned themselves towards her arms, legs, torso, and head. First came the gauntlets as they enveloped her forearms, followed by the armor applied to her legs. Next up was the chest and backplates, which clamped around her upper body. Finally, the helmet fit over her head, but not before the nanotech wrapped themselves around her neck and cranium, leaving only her chin, mouth, and nose exposed.

To compensate for her long hair, the nanomachines formed around it to create a makeshift ponytail. Once the helmet was placed on her scalp, the accompanying visor blocked her vision from the outside world.

After the attachment was placed, she started hearing soft, high-pitched sounds coming from her backplate. Ramona had seen Eric put on the suit enough times to recognize that it was the transparent tubes that would extend from the wearer's back to each limb attachment. The battery that powered the pilot suit was stored in the backplate and required the tubes to power the four extremity attachments.

Meanwhile, a separate battery powered the complex mechanisms of the visor, which remained unattached to the rest of the suit. Together, both the nanotech and outfit could allow the pilot to dictate the giant robot's movements while also transmitting direct feedback to the user. This primarily involved the latter's sense of touch, sight, and hearing. By the time everything was set, the visor activated, displaying a wide empty room composed of a serene blue void.

"Alright then, things aren't gonna be as easy as it was for the kid when I got him into shape since we unfortunately don't have the time. For the first part of our crash course, we're gonna get you accustomed to basic movements. Just focus on your wits and fists."

Ramona nodded in eager determination. "Okay, let's do this."

The AI activated a virtual recreation of Acapulco. While she never had the chance to experience the popular tourist destination, Ramona was familiar enough with how the city looked from photos and videos. She was enthralled by how accurate the simulation looked. In addition to her surroundings, there was a projection that enwrapped her whole body. One in the shape of Draco Azul's familiar silhouette. Ramona couldn't help but feel impressed by how much detail Ekchuah put into making the experience as authentic as possible. Even her own movements felt slightly slower and heavier as the simulation mimicked the weight of mech's immense size and weight. She started wondering if this sensation was how piloting the real thing truly was.

In front of her, the model of a Diablo rendered into shape. As the figure's texture started rendering its overall appearance became clear. It appeared to be a giant, turquoise-colored amphibious creature with a humanoid build and scaly skin. It reminded Ramona of an old horror film she used to watch with her father when she was a little girl. She then recognized the titanic creature as one of the first Diablo to appear following the start of Diablo invasion, having caught the fight on television. Suddenly, Ekchuah's voice began blaring from all around her like an invisible spectator.

"This one's perfect for a rookie like you since it's sheer brute strength. But be wary of its speed 'cause this guy's quicker than you'd think."

"Got it!"

The battle began as Ramona and the aquatic behemoth dashed towards each other. Immediately grappling one another, each combatant attempted to overpower the other. Unfortunately, the Diablo had the upper hand in raw strength and started overwhelming her. Ramona countered with a fierce knee to the aquatic monster's ribs multiple times, her spiked armor penetrating the beast's flesh. The creature's grip loosened, allowing her to grab its face with her left hand and slam her right hand into its razor-sharp maw.

Then the skilled fighter followed up with an additional high kick to the Diablo's already dazed cranium. Despite her best efforts, the creature still stood, albeit with a few missing teeth. The giant proved to be more resilient than she thought.

Rather than submitting, the monster lifted a small building and threw it at the metal warrior. Instinctively, Ramona blocked the incoming structure. The edifice smashed into thousands of pieces against her virtually indestructible exterior as if it was made of brittle plastic. As she lowered her arms, her gaze was met by a scaly fist. Ramona reared back from the jolt of pain. It felt every bit as painful as the real thing. Taking advantage of the moment, the amphibious monster threw jab after jab to the young woman's face. Ramona lifted her arms to give her some reprieve from the creature's brutality as it kept striking.

Remembering her mech's arm blades, she aimed them at her opponent, causing the unearthly titan to slice its own hands in the middle of its blind fury. She then pushed away the Diablo. Once she found a brief moment to catch her breath, the pilot wiped her face and checked for blood, unaware that such an act was pointless when all she could see is Draco Azul's hand scrapping against its mouth plate.

Infuriated, Ramona launched an uppercut right into the creature's jaw, which allowed the Diablo to grab hold of Ramona's arm with its surprisingly fast reflexes. The fish man spun around and tossed her into one of the virtual houses nearby. Ramona took a rough landing as she collided with the small neighborhood. She felt the broken concrete and metal collide with her body. The gilled menace roared out to its downed enemy.

As he watched the fight progress, Ekchuah worried over Ramona. She was a skilled brawler, but when Eric first fought the Diablo, it too was very proficient in hand-to-hand combat. Ramona had to switch things up if she had a chance of piloting Draco Azul, let alone using it against the Nagual. She needed to adapt to different strategies.

"Ramona! If you're gonna win, you need to focus. Think outside the box if you have to. It's gonna take more than simple kicks and punches to bring a Diablo down."

Still dazed, the young woman shook her head, coughing as she laid on the broken streets. Ramona found that assertion ironic as she made a similar statement to Eric when they trained. She started to realize just how difficult it was to maintain concentration when under the control of Draco Azul. On top of adjusting to the speed, strength, and weight of the robot, she now needed to pay close attention to an unorthodox enemy in an equally surreal arena. It was then that she sympathized with Eric's constant ordeals.

However, the AI was right. If she was going to successfully pilot the giant robot, she had to work smarter, not harder. Ramona wasn't some unskilled thug off the street that relied on brute force. She was raised by one of the best fighters she knew, her father. As the girl looked back on her training one memory suddenly surged in her mind: a very precious one, in fact.

When she was a little girl, Ramona and her father bonded over Mexican professional wrestling, known locally as lucha libre. The mask-wearing fighters she grew up with specialized in rapid sequences of holds and maneuvers that could pummel foes. On top of that, they were able to jump to great heights as if they were flying around the ring. Those televised bouts were what motivated her into convincing her father to teach her how to fight.

While the strategies of professional wrestling lacked practical functionality in real life, she used to practice certain techniques with her father for fun before graduating to more serious means of combat. Having remembered what her father taught her, Ramona stood up and took a deep breath.

"Apá, I hope you're watching right now," spoke Ramona in her native language as she performed the sign of the cross for good luck.

Finally near its target, the fish-like monster launched another barrage of fists. This time, the young woman avoided the blows and grabbed the Diablo's left wrist. Ramona stepped in front of the beast and yanked the arm upwards to restrict its movement. She twisted the forearm as intensely as she could. This new form of stress irritated the Diablo. It swatted at her with its other arm, but Ramona maneuvered around it while still maintaining her grip. After applying immense amounts of pressure, the young woman heard a bone snap followed by the screams of the Diablo. When Ramona finally released her hold, the amphibious beast withdrew to tend to its injured arm.

The tables had turned, and Ramona could not waste any more precious time. She had to defeat this creature and move ahead with her training. Squeezing her arms around the beast's waist, the young warrior lifted him up with every ounce of Draco Azul's strength before throwing the scaly monstrosity back down on the streets of downtown Acapulco. As its back impacted the solid ground with a thunderous slam, the Diablo shrieked in pain, its spine and muscles in sheer agony. Surging through its body was a pain unlike anything it had ever experienced. Ramona stood tall against her opponent. Playing right into her trap, the Diablo reached out for her leg with his one good arm.

She twisted herself into a second standing arm lock, ready to break the other limb. While trying to stand, the creature also attempted to shake Ramona off, but the young woman held on for dear life. Finally, she heard another cracking sound. The weight and strength of the massive robot was enough to successfully shatter the other arm. With no real means of defense, the gilled menace was rendered incapacitated. In a last act of defiance, the Diablo viciously chomped down on the automaton's right ankle as she stood up.

"Agh!" she screamed out.

Ramona rained blows down on the scaly abomination's skull until it finally released its ferocious grip.

"¡Esto lo vas a pagar!" Ramona vengefully yelled out to her opponent.

While she recouped from her sustained injuries, Ramona could not help but think of the situation she, Ekchuah, and Eric found themselves in. It had been strenuous for her watching both her friends and innocent people suffer. If there was any good moment to cut loose and let out all her frustrations, now would be the time. She was ready to finish off this facsimile of what she would be confronting soon.

The determined woman clutched the Diablo by his throat, robbing the aquatic terror of all oxygen. Instinctively, the monster wrangled side to side as would an alligator, but Ramona struck its chest with vindictive bladed blows. The scaly giant tried to muster all the strength he could to move its arms to stop the inevitable. Alas, it was futile as Draco Azul's bladed fist sliced through the beast's torso, shattering its sternum, and finally piercing the Diablo's weakening heart. By the time the pilot let go of the gargantuan fish-man's throat, the Diablo laid motionless. In seconds, the monster's body faded out of sight into ones and zeros.

Test number one was complete, and Ramona had passed with flying colors. Her face had some bruises from the abuse taken by the aquatic nightmare, but she smiled, having experienced far worse in the past. She looked all around her at the now disappearing landscape. Frowning, the trainee warrior examined the destroyed landmarks. If this had been a real fight, countless people would have been lost forever. Ekchuah noticed her concern.

"You did well for a first-timer," he remarked in an attempt to console her.

"Sure, but what about the people of Acapulco?"

"Things never work out exactly as planned. You can't save everyone," Ekchuah said. "Eric found that out the hard way, as does every pilot, eventually. But that's why we're here."

"Y-yeah, alright," Ramona replied, still unsure if she could improve enough to save everyone. Yet, such doubts were not going to help her. The lives of everyone were in her hands and she needed to push out such useless thoughts. "What's next?"

"Alright, this time we're going to focus on the Draco Fangs, but you're not going to be hacking and slashing all willy-nilly."

Ramona raised an eyebrow, wondering what Ekchuah meant by that. Around her the arena changed to a location she was less familiar with. It was an oceanside city with a naval base in the distance. Yet, it did not look like any city she was familiar with in southern Mexico.

"What is this place?" asked the curious pilot.

"This here is Ensenada, near the U.S. border."

Suddenly, Ramona's feet felt the ground shake as a new Diablo erupted from the street below her. This one resembled a cross between a crustacean and a scorpion. Its armored body was adorned with ten limbs, eight arms and two massive legs, each ending in crab-like claws. The back of its greenish blue exoskeleton extended outwards, resembling large fins like those of a manta ray. The sea creature had a long, segmented tail with what appeared to be a stinger at the end. Topping off the grotesque body was a horrific face decorated with two pairs of serrated mandibles and menacing orange eyes that beamed at Ramona in a haunting fashion. It was unlike anything she had ever seen up to this point.

Taking advantage of a dazed Ramona, the Diablo rushed in for the first blow and struck at her with all eight pincers. With how accurately the attack was aimed, grabbing all four of her limbs simultaneously, Ramona felt every bit of the assault at once. All she could respond with were screams of agony. Out of desperation, Ramona tried jamming her bladed arm into the monster invertebrate's face. It ducked its head to the side, instead catching the attack with its neck. Her weapon did not dig deep into the shelled carapace of her enemy, but it was enough for the Diablo to let go of its prey from the temporary shock of counterattack. As it backed off it generated loud clicking noises.

A powerful crimson laser fired from the crustaceous monster's stinger. Ramona took notice and used her arms to block the shot. The force of the beam was too much for her to handle. It pushed the giant automaton backwards onto the streets, leaving behind a straight crevice. Dazed, Ramona saw the crustacean charging its beam attack again. She leaped out of the laser's reach and hid behind a building for temporary cover. The young woman peeked her head out from behind the structure, without being noticed, to see if any damage was done. Ramona expected to see some damage on the creature from when she struck it. Rather, its neck only carried a barely visible gash left by her blade.

She realized that physical attacks would not work on this new opponent. The battle was now a deadly game of cat and mouse. Ramona needed to find a chink in the Diablo's impenetrable armor. The young woman did consider using the Draco Striker. However, she knew that it would take a lot of time to charge, time she was sure the monstrosity would not allow. The young fighter stared at the blades, unscathed by the energy discharge while Draco Azul's metal sizzled in intense heat. She wondered if the beam could injure its user if it was reflected back at it.

"I know what you're thinking," the AI cheekily said. "Shout out the phrase 'Draco Fangs' to use them as handheld weapons."

Ramona grinned before taking a deep breath.

"Draco Fangs!"

In mere moments, the blades launched into the air and instinctively, the former knife wielder grasped the pair of massive sabers. Holding each one in a reverse grip fashion, much like her previous weapon of choice, she peeked her head out to see where the Diablo currently was. It was laying waste to the city in its voracious intent to slaughter Ensenada's entire population. It clearly did not have much of an attention span, Ramona thought.

She then stepped out of hiding and ran towards the leviathan. Before the creature took notice, Ramona stretched her right arm back and threw the giant blade as hard as she could. It spun in the air, approaching its target with great speed. Her throw resulted in a direct hit. Upon impact, the sword wedged itself into the armored beast's back.

The Diablo did not scream or even seem to feel pain. Rather, it turned around as a red illumination lit up the spot where the blade had made contact. Then the ambient crimson glow passed down its spine and charged into its tail. Knowing what was to come, Ramona gripped her remaining sword tightly. This was how it projected its lasers, she thought. Any physical attack directed at the monster gets converted into energy.

Then the invertebrate shot another beam of intense heat. The young woman successfully blocked it with her left blade. As Ramona took the brunt of the laser, she noticed that this blast was much less intense than the monster's previous attack. Slowly, she pushed forward to redirect the projectile. Once the stream of energy died down, a plan hatched inside her mind. Quickly moving Draco Azul close enough to the Diablo, she reached for the lodged Draco

121

Fang, landing a kick on the armored menace's back to pry the sword loose.

Such a forceful move stirred the inner workings of the abomination. The impact left by her attack was just what it needed to transfer that kinetic energy into another blast from its tail. A loud screech and one charge session later, the fiend shot one more energy projection at Ramona. With both blades in hand, she mustered as much strength as she could to block the attack, its power now stronger than before. Slowly, she repositioned both blades as a means of redirecting back at her opponent. At last, she rebounded the titanic arthropod's laser as its skin was penetrated by the ruby-colored beam. By the time the beam died down, the creature's left arms and fin had been sliced clean off, leaving its soft organs and muscles exposed to the outside world.

"Now's your chance to finish it off," Ekchuah announced. "Chant the phrase 'Draco,' concentrate on your target, then scream 'Striker' to bring the pain!'"

Ramona followed her teacher's words exactly as she was told.

"Draco…!'"

The moment she recited the first half of Draco Azul's ultimate finisher, her vision shifted to that of a target and reticle, as well as a meter that signified how much energy she was charging up. She could sense her entire body vibrating as electricity surged towards her forehead. This was the robot's ability to summon forth all of its usable energy and weaponize it into its most devastating attack. The creature before her was in too much pain to move out of the way. For the Diablo, escape was impossible.

"Striker!"

At last, she finished the incantation and unleashed a torrent of lightning at the monster. A gigantic explosion erupted as the Diablo was vaporized in an instant. Simulated blood and guts poured down on the virtual city and on herself. Ramona brushed off the viscera that got onto her metal avatar. She carefully walked around the streets in search for any signs of the arthropod. All that was left of her ruthless opponent was its destroyed remains.

Ramona breathed heavily, relieved the second bout was at an end. The young woman was about to call out to Ekchuah for them to move on, before her vision started to blur. Suddenly, the world around her spun before she collapsed to the ground. On her hands and knees, she caught vague glimpses the simulation dissipating as the session ended. Sapped of all her strength, it wasn't long before she fell unconscious.

***

The young woman woke up some time later. She found herself in her normal clothes, only now she was laying on a fold-out bed attached to one of the cockpit's walls. Before her, stood Ekchuah.

"You were out for about fifteen minutes," he explained with concern in his voice. "How are you holding up?"

"I-I'm fine. How's Eric?"

"Heh. He's still the same," chuckled Ekchuah, amused by the lady's ability to put the health and safety of others over her own. Perhaps she did have it in her to pull this off, thought the AI. "But you need to worry about yourself."

"This is nothing. Let's move on," suggested Ramona as she got out of bed and back on her feet. However, the moment her legs made impact, her dizziness started to return. She gripped the bed tightly to hold her balance.

"Despite being a simulation, the pressure you feel from Draco Azul's power is, in fact, real. Now that we know what your limit is, we'll have to refrain from using the Draco Striker, otherwise you'll be a goner."

Ramona now understood why Eric was always winded after every fight. She wondered how many trials he had to endure before he could finish a fight without succumbing to fatigue. Still, with everything on the line, she dejected what limits she had to work with.

"Fair enough. Now, let's continue."

"Ramona, the last thing we need is our only hope to beat the Nagual to die from over exhaustion. You need to rest," Ekchuah protested, noticing the toll the simulation had taken on Ramona.

Her face was drenched in sweat. Yet her body shook as she forced herself to push onward. She let go of the bed and stood tall once more.

"That's why we need to do this, otherwise more people will die," countered Ramona. "I am not going to risk all that over a little rest. Now, give me the next challenge!"

Ekchuah sighed as the AI wondered how much Ramona was actually capable of handling.

"As you wish. This'll be the last one and the most challenging. If you can pass this, you'll be ready."

Ramona smiled and confidently gave a thumbs up.

CHAPTER 12

With the bar-owner-turned-pilot back in the simulation, the final scenario began to render itself. Ramona recognized this new environment as she actually witnessed this location firsthand very recently, Chihuahua City. She knew exactly what Ekchuah had in mind for her. Once the battlefield had finished populating around her, her rival was the next to be loaded.

The being had two heads, one resembling a wild boar and the other was a beaked, bird-like cranium that resided on the behemoth's chest. It had two pairs of pure black eyes, a coating of reddish-brown feathers, and a lengthy tail. Ramona remembered the beast that stood in front of her all too well. It was the same two-headed Diablo that Eric fought before everything went downhill with the Nagual.

"Because the Nagual used this Diablo's blood to power his army, there's no doubt their strength will be comparable to this creature," the bodiless voice of Ekchuah exposited.

"Got it. Just one thing," exclaimed Ramona.

"Yeah?"

"Do any of these Diablos have actual names?"

Surprised, Ekchuah had to pause for a second before responding, never thinking about the subject until now.

"I mean, we suspect these creatures come from space. So, they must've had some kind of designation wherever they came from. The only time we learned of one was when a plant-like Diablo called 'Rozacdyl' attacked Durango City. That was not too far from here, actually. But we only knew that because we were aided by an alien bounty hunter who was familiar with the species."

"Wait, an alien bounty hunter?" said a bewildered Ramona.

"Oh, I'll tell you all about that another time. But to answer your question, no. We don't have any names for them on record."

"Have you ever thought of giving them names?"

"The thing is, Eric and I never saw it necessary to give them names. I just store their data in Draco's memory banks. If we ever need to refer to a past Diablo, all I need to do is dig through the files based on the time and location of its appearance and presto, we have a recreation."

Seeing the scarlet Diablo now standing in front of her, Ramona conceded, having her curiosity satiated for the time being. The story of the extraterrestrial ally certainly intrigued her, however.

"Good enough for me. Now let's get things started!" said Ramona, mimicking the words Ekchuah used at the start of their training.

Making the first move, the feathered beast fired its dual plasma beams at the metal giant, but its pilot dodged and attempted a knee strike to the lower head just as her predecessor did. Given their previous encounter with the creature, Ramona remembered that its heads were crucial vital points. Cut one down and it can still fight, but once both are disposed of the Diablo would be no more. The creature, however, grasped her mobile leg and crushed the armor surrounding it.

Excruciating, the simulated pain humbled her for a moment before regaining her senses. In retaliation, she stabbed at the humongous demon, but it relinquished its hold before any damage could have been done.

In that moment, the simulation froze, with the Diablo standing in place. Ekchuah's voice was heard once more.

"I notice that you've yet to use your scarf. How about we see how well you can move it."

"How do I do that?" asked Ramona.

"Think of it like a third arm, imagine it reaching out in front of you. Like you're grabbing an orange from a tree."

Using this moment of silence, she placed all her thoughts on moving the scarf wrapped around her virtual avatar's neck. Slowly, she felt the fabric shift underneath her chin. She then noticed the red cloth rising, twitching and flickering about like a lit flame. Beads of sweat were now pouring down her forehead. Thankfully, the nanotech suit absorbed every ounce of perspiration so as to keep her comfortable. Yet still, she struggled getting the scarf to reach out.

"That's enough," ordered the AI. "Clearly that's something we're not gonna have ready in time for the Nagual."

"Gah!" Ramona gasped as she lost her concentration, the cloth falling limp as a result. "How does Eric even do this?"

"It comes natural for some pilots, other times it doesn't. It could be that since Eric never learned to fight until we met, he got accustomed to fighting with an extra limb. You on the other hand already have years under your belt. You're almost too accustomed to your own style."

"You're kidding," said the annoyed trainee.

"Ah, don't worry about it. Everyone gets it eventually. But hey, don't let that stop you. There are still more uses for the scarf. Remember what I said, you gotta think outside the box. Now that you know all the basics, it's time for you to start fighting like a true pilot. You've got guts, but don't rely on just your own strengths this time. Learn to rely on Draco's as well. Now go get 'em!"

"Got it, coach." Ramona paused for a second as she realized what she just said. Was she turning into Eric?

As she kept Ekchuah's last words in mind, the simulation came back to life. Once more, the crimson monster was on the assault. Utilizing what she learned from her fight with the amphibious Diablo, Ramona advanced towards her opponent at top speed. She remembered that Draco Azul has strength far disproportional to that of a man. Leaping into the sky with the mech's massive legs, she sailed over her adversary until she landed behind it. Taking the beast by surprise, the lady locked the top head in a tight sleeper hold from behind, while avoiding the lower one.

The creature clawed at the robot's arms all while it struck back with a thunderous whip of its long feathery tail. Ramona was knocked back from momentum but kept her balance stable so as not to lose her footing. At a critical moment, the mammalian beast tackled her while ensnaring the mech within its muscular bicep, knocking the pilot down to the ground. Leering down at her from above, the beast charged up its dreaded projectile attack. The young woman rolled out of the way to put some distance between herself and the creature as it blasted the ground beneath it.

"Draco Fang!"

In that instant, Ramona launched one of the arm blades at her enemy. The monster dodged just fast enough to escape a direct hit to its torso. However, its tail was sliced into at the midpoint by the flying saber. To her disbelief, the two-headed beast did not flinch as it picked up the cold piece of alien metal with its sharp claws.

"No la hagas," said the annoyed pilot.

Just then, the female warrior remembered the scarf she had been unable to properly utilize. Now was the moment of truth. She could not have it reach out to grab the metaphorical orange on its own. But with her own strength, perhaps it could.

Ramona manipulated Draco Azul into grabbing onto its scarf. She then had the robot swing the garment in a circular pattern, building momentum as it twirled around. Finally, she threw the scarf forward, imagining it wrapping around the blade in the behemoth's hand. At last, it followed her command. Shocked, the beast struggled to loosen the cloth's tight hold. Before the creature could pry the scarf loose, Ramona forcefully pulled the crimson cloth and the blade tore free from the Diablo's hand, leaving a deep gash in its palm.

Unfortunately, the maneuver came at a cost as the Draco Fang was pointed right back at its wielder, having slipped from the scarf's grip the moment Ramona lost concentration. The young woman ducked, letting the giant bayonet collide with a nearby hotel building behind her. She swore under her breath in frustration. Being an opportunist, the aberration swatted at Ramona. She bypassed each strike, beginning to read the creature's moves. However, the effects of piloting Draco Azul were catching up to her. The stamina she gained from her brief rest was nearly depleted, giving the Diablo the chance to rake her torso with one misstep.

"Gaaah!" Ramona cried out.

Draco Azul now had three long, digitally simulated scars from its shoulder blades to the bottom of what would be its rib cage. Once more, the pain felt as lifelike as it could be.

In a knee-jerk reaction, Ramona jumped up into the air once more. Using extra airtime from the mech's massive leap, she twisted her body forward into a spinning motion. She had never attempted such a move before, but always imagined performing this technique having grown up on the bevy of Japanese superhero shows that aired on Mexican television. With her body in position, she brought down a heel kick directly into the Diablo's top skull. The creature tried grabbing her leg in anticipation, but the speed and weight of the attack was too much for the double-headed terror. Both combatants landed on the ground with a thunderous impact.

The 27-year-old felt motion sickness from the constant spinning. As she shook off her nausea, Ramona caught the Diablo getting back up from the corner of her eye.

"Draco Fang!"

Concentrating on her remaining blade, she launched the weapon like a boomerang and sliced off one of the Diablo's arms. The menace screeched in raw fury. Ramona took this opportunity to look back at what the first Draco Fangs was wedged into. The Diablo lunged at her with its remaining left arm. Taking evasive action, she backed herself toward the hotel and pulled the blade from where it was lodged.

Wailing, and throwing a child-like tantrum by smashing anything nearby with its one good hand, the tusked and beaked nightmare went on a wild rampage. The young woman at last saw an opening to exploit its Achilles heel. Now that she was finally able to do some damage to the enemy, Ramona needed to further target the heads without being on the receiving end of its rampage.

Once Draco Azul stepped forward, landing a mighty stomp to the earth below, the manic demon turned its attention to the commotion and recognized its enemy once more. Right as it was about to charge towards the battle-ready Ramona, a familiar scarlet beam zipped past her defenses and struck the woman's right hip. She jumped out of the laser's firing range, but the damage was done. The injured warrior rubbed her upper leg to ease the seething tension as she was left utterly befuddled. Ramona looked all around for where the laser came from. Her curiosity was answered as she heard two familiar roars, one loud as a lion and the other as shrill as nails on a chalkboard.

"Really?"

"If we're gonna be ready to fight multiple targets, this is the way to go," the AI said.

"Sure, but this soon?"

"Hey, I said we didn't have much time. This is your last test!"

Stepping out of the shadows, Ramona saw a familiar scaly and finned face. It was the humanoid fish monster from the first battle. Beside it was the crab-like entity that was responsible for burning her leg. The turquoise Diablo bashed on his shelled ally, allowing it to charge the kinetic energy into another blast. Ramona narrowly avoided the attack, only to find both the red and blue monsters chasing her down. The aquatic being closed the distance between them at a much faster rate, trying to bite her face off. Nimbly, the lady evaded every swipe and chomp.

Seizing an opportunity to inflict some damage, Ramona used her Draco Fang to slice at the Diablo's chest, forcing the amphibious beast to back off. Watching from a distance, the two-headed demon fired at Draco Azul from behind.

Little did the crimson monstrosity know, Ramona had led the pair towards the location of the missing blade she had thrown earlier. She ducked down to avoid the titan's plasma strikes while simultaneously acquiring her second blade from the ground. With beams of energy colliding with the giant gillman, she used the moment of confusion to plunge both blades into the lower head of the feathered creature. The avian cranium twitched and screeched in pain until, at last, it was silenced by death's grip.

Immediately afterwards, the aquatic brute retaliated, its chest scarred by its ally's attack. Ramona, running on fumes by that point, was growing tired of this never-ending madness. Still attached to her blades, the pilot lifted the enemy and threw it as a makeshift projectile. The two massive titans collided and tumbled over one another. By now, the final opponent had caught up with the trio.

Ekchuah had intentionally placed Ramona into a situation similar to the one she would have to confront when she eventually faced the Nagual and his followers. They would not be playing fair, and Ramona had to know what it would be like to face multiple opponents at once. This ensured that she would be prepared for vampires or any other demonic atrocities she encountered while piloting the mighty azure colossus alongside her friend.

The living hologram employed similar strategies with Eric when he had previously trained him. Still, Ramona was getting infuriated as the training prolonged. These past challenges were tough enough, but this was proving to be nearly impossible. One violent Diablo was adequately difficult, but three of them back to back? Despite nearing the last of her reserves, she could not give up, not when the world was at stake. Ramona was dead set on taking them all on.

She stared down at each giant. On her right was the crab, to her left was the fish-man, and lastly the feathered beast, with only its top head remaining, stood before her. Each atrocity went at the young woman all at once with their claws, maws, and pincers ready to tear her to shreds. Ramona clenched her fists around her blood-soaked sabers and crossed her arms in an x-shaped pose. She was thus preparing the mech's strongest move in its arsenal.

"Draco…!"

"No!" interrupted Ekchuah.

The holographic mentor finally decided to step in by stopping the simulation a second time. "I told you, you're not ready for that!"

"What other choice do I have?" Ramona protested, blinded by fury as she lowered her arms.

Ekchuah knew for a fact this suicidal tactic would never work on all three monsters at once. The AI needed to calm her down before she made a crucial mistake.

"The Draco Striker has range, but not enough to catch all three at once. Say you get at least two. What are you going to do when that last Diablo comes at ya and you're passed out?"

Ramona stood silent, unsure where her mentor was getting at.

"It's times like these where you gotta improvise," Ekchuah continued. "That's something Eric often did when his back was up against the wall. Like I said before, you have the tools at your disposal. Use them!"

Ramona calmed down. Her heart rate lowered as she examined her surroundings. The trio of horrific beasts began to move once more, surrounding her like football players about to tackle a running back. The pilot mentally commanded Draco Azul to jump away, forcing the Diablos to gather together as they all ran in front of her. She threw one of the blades at the crowd. The Diablos separated to avoid the sharp, swinging piece of metal. In response, the crab and bird veered to her right while the fish moved to the left.

With the scaly giant isolated, she grabbed her scarf and twirled it at the enemy's neck. As soon as the creature was caught in the cloth's suffocating grip, Ramona pulled the scarf, lifting the beast off its feet and sent him crashing into the crab and bird. The moment the gillman got up, she tugged the monster towards her before stabbing him right in the chest. The beast screamed in pain as the blade sliced down his already wounded torso, leaking the Diablo's blood and guts to the soil below. Before the monster could retaliate, its head was lopped clean off its shoulders with the very same weapon.

One down, two to go, Ramona told herself.

Watching the slaughter unfold, the formerly two-headed behemoth prepared another blast of energy while the arthropod burrowed underground. The feathered beast fired at its enemy while the crab disappeared from sight. Feeling the earth shake beneath her feet, the young woman jumped up in the air as the shellfish erupted from the ground. Consequently, the arthropodal threat was hit with the full force of the plasma fireball, which was just what it needed to unleash another searing laser. By the time Ramona landed, the crustacean fired off its own stream of energy.

Ramona directed Draco Azul to run as fast as it could away from the beam, directing it instead to the feathered freak. The pilot leapt over the surprised creature and held it in place as the laser bore through its torso. Its mammalian-like skull melted by the second before the scarlet beam fried the layer of bones and organs underneath. Decreasing in intensity, the energy emitting from the crab's tail died down before it could penetrate through to the robot. By then the bird was nothing more than a smoldering corpse.

The death of its two compatriots warranted zero reaction to the already enraged invertebrate. As it had all but run out of kinetic energy to assault Draco Azul with, it began one last Hail Mary charge at the mechanical warrior. Ramona noticed her vision starting to blur once again. She could not pull off a Draco Striker even if she tried. The young woman then remembered where the first Draco Fang landed when she initially split up the group.

Wielding her crimson scarf one last time, she aimed it at the lone blade stuck in the remains of a small restaurant. Immediately, she pulled on the weapon and aimed its trajectory at the beast who was about to eviscerate her mech with its multiple pincers. The Draco Fang embedded itself deep into the back of the crab's neck. Unfortunately, it was not enough to finish off the giant scorpion-crab hybrid. It crashed into the mech as it pushed Ramona into a series of resorts behind her.

Ramona could feel each claw grapple her armor and its double jaws latched to her face. The determined warrior had become so fatigued that she had grown numb to the pain. As she pushed back against the onslaught of crustaceous limbs, Ramona managed to free her one arm and grabbed onto the blade stuck in the creature's elongated neck.

With all of her might, she pulled at the weapon, each tug bringing the saber further and further down. Feeling itself, the crab attempted to stop the torturous process. Its mandibles let go of Draco Azul's face and aimed for the arm, only to have its maxillae blocked as another blade was jammed inside its mouth. By releasing its grip, the monster had freed the mech just enough for it to seal the beast's fate. One last yank was all it took to sever the connection between the monster's head and the rest of its gruesome carapace.

The creature slumped over its rival; however, she was incapable of lifting the dead opponent off her. Though this mattered not for Ramona for she had won.

Fortunately, the pressure of the massive corpse did not last long, for it began to wither away along with Ramona's entire surrounding. This signaled to her that the virtual simulation had ended. Without a moment's hesitation, she yanked off the visor as she gasped one massive breath of fresh air.

"Amazing work!" said Ekchuah as he gave her an enthusiastic thumbs up.

Ramona returned the gesture while she wiped her face with a towel handed to her by a mechanical appendage.

"Thanks," responded the lady before she fell silent.

"What's wrong?" asked the AI as he noticed his new pupil staring at her towel.

"That's strange, there's no blood. Just sweat."

"Why would there be? It was only a simulation."

"Yeah, but it felt so real. I was getting murdered out there!"

The AI chuckled as he gestured at the woman's suit. "That's the point. This whole system is meant to simulate pain by having the suit tap into your pain receptors. Though, it'll never actually kill you. Not in a million years!"

Ramona was at a loss for words. The young lady thought she would have actually lost her life if she were to have been defeated by the trifecta of monsters. Perhaps, she thought, Ekchuah refrained from telling her to put her in the exact state of mind she needed to be in for when she eventually faced off against the Nagual. Having experienced a life and death struggle, maybe then she was not only physically ready to handle the terrible ghouls, but psychologically as well.

"But now, it's time for the real deal," Ekchuah stated. "After you take a breather, of course."

The warrior sighed, nervous at the thought of resting as more lives were offered to the Nagual and his army of mindless zombies. Yet, he was right. If she just jumped into battle now, the newly battle-worn woman would fail to beat the vampire.

"Give me ten minutes to get a drink, but we're going right after," Ramona told Ekchuah.

"You're getting thirty!" The AI smirked while she sat down in the chair she used when Eric would fight as she was handed a bottle of ice-cold water to cool down by another mechanical appendage.

"Alright, coach."

CHAPTER 13

Draco Azul's golden eyes shined as they reflected the last few rays of daylight from the setting sun. The blue colossus's wing's folded outwards and its engines roared, ready to take flight. Lifting its head, the titanic machine rocketed into the skies before propelling its body forward. Its destination: Chihuahua City.

Inside, Ekchuah handled the mech via autopilot while Ramona took her time preparing for the battle that lay ahead. Fortunately, the AI could manage to manipulate Draco Azul just as long as he did not have to also take up combat like last night. The cockpit's artificial gravity activated, allowing Ramona to stand upright with ease as the mech laid horizontal within the clouds.

"We'll be there shortly. Remember, once we reach the ground it's all up to you," the hologram told his newest protégé.

Ramona didn't respond verbally. Rather, she acknowledged his words with a nod as she geared up, a nutrition bar hanging in her mouth. As the nanotech suit covered her body, all she could think of was finally finishing off the Nagual once and for all, saving everyone in the process, Eric especially. On screen, the monitors in the cockpit revealed what had befallen the once vibrant city. Chihuahua burned, its buildings engulfed in a blazing inferno. All that the robot's audio sensors could pick up were civilians screaming in horror and pleading for help as hundreds of ghouls screeched in rage and bloodlust.

Rage percolating inside her, Ramona clenched her fist in sheer fury. Witnessing all this carnage reminded her of when her hometown was devastated by two horrific Diablos. She could still remember the devils smashing her inherited home and business to smithereens. The young woman recalled the destruction they laid before Eric and Draco Azul ultimately saved the day. There was not much the former bar owner could do to stop the abhorrent threats back then, but things had now changed. Inspired by their valiant heroics, she had made it her mission to assist Eric and Ekchuah any way she could.

Now Ramona could finally step forward and pull her own weight as a member of this rag tag trio. The Nagual was going to pay for all the lives that he stole. Draco Azul descended to the urban wasteland below with a deafening boom. The streets shuddered under the metallic titan's feet.

In the cockpit, Ramona waited for the ghouls to take notice of the impact of her not-so-subtle entrance. In less than a few seconds, she and Ekchuah heard bird-like screeches and canine snarls surrounding them. All around the mech they could see hundreds of ghouls perched atop every building and house in the area. Each one of them kept their distance, forming a mile wide radius around the gigantic challenger. Many had mutated into bird, bat, and wolf-esque forms akin to those that Ramona and Eric had encountered before.

They all howled, screeched, and hissed at the giant mecha, sounding like an audience at the Roman coliseum demanding the execution of a failed gladiator. None were intimidated by the towering form of Draco Azul this time around, which told its pilot that they all must be under the control of the alien menace. She wondered how much time Eric had left before he would be just as they were: feral, hungry, and inhuman.

As if on cue, the demonic zombie minions converged on the mech. They all grew to thirty times their size, rivaling that of Draco Azul. They each contained the ability to match the robot in scale, much like the beast-man that had previously tested this new ability. Yet, it appeared that around twenty had grown to full size as many more were only half of the Primal Warrior's height, while the rest kept their original statures. Ramona mused that perhaps not all of them had the strength to endure such a transformation. However, the reason behind the monsters' inconsistent growth was of no concern to her. While they could match her in power, she was certain she had strategy on her side.

The pilot performed a sign of the cross, asking for forgiveness for the lives she was ready to take, before releasing the left blade from her arm and sending it into her grasp. She quickly wrapped the blade in the mech's long blood-red scarf around its handle. Inside, Ramona anticipated the mob of vampiric abominations with her newly readied technique. From the skies above, owl-like creatures both giant and small were the first to reach the robot. On ground level, a pack of wolf-men sprinted on all fours towards the humanoid machine.

Draco Azul swung its saber at the first wave of vicious canines while still attached to the cloth. Overhead, the owl and bat-men rained down on the metallic goliath. One owl-man in particular was closer than any of its brethren, ready to rip its enemy to shreds with its massive talons. The azure giant grabbed the end of its scarf as its pilot took in a deep breath. Having tried a primitive version of this technique in the simulation, Ramona decided it was time to perfect it on the battlefield.

"This is the viper's strike, Draco Víbora!" Ramona confidently announced.

The mech swung the bladed weapon like a massive flail at one of the giant owls. Its wide arc cleaved the ghoul in two at its feathered abdomen. Ramona kept the momentum of the blade going for several more swings at the following winged demons. One hurl decapitated a bat-man, with another sliced off another owl-man's right wing. Finally, one more launch of the blade lopped off a second bat-men's legs. Each fallen foe tumbled around the mechanical soldier followed by their dismembered body parts.

"Keep it up!" encouraged Ekchuah. "Lucky for us, these guys don't seem as smart as ol' Wolf-boy! They'll keep blindingly charging at us in the hope that they can wear you down."

"But we won't let that happen!" remarked the new pilot with a smile.

"Attagirl!"

Once the larger enemies were disposed of, Ramona took notice of the smaller winged beasts closing in. She manipulated the sapphire defender into twirling the roped blade into a circular pattern above its head. Using it like a razor-sharp fan, the swinging saber shredded every one of the airborne ghouls. All that was left of them was a mist of red paste that showered the upper body of the giant automaton. Two more of the Diablo-sized abominations soared down from both sides, talons and claws ready to pierce the mech's stained armor.

Draco Azul lashed the blade out at one of the creatures and impaled the owl-man square in its chest. It yanked the devil downwards into the ground and spun in place to toss its body into its giant, chiropteran brethren. The mighty robot then slammed its foot down and crushed the bat's head into a bloody pulp.

Rising in volume were the snarls and howls of the giant wolf-men and ghouls as they grew closer. Still stuck on the makeshift flail, the pierced and battered remains of the barely living owl-man were sent flying once more before being smashed against the first waves of the Nagual's grounded minions. The mech quickened its spinning technique, allowing the battered cadaver to slide off and collide with the next batch of giant-sized wolf-men. Removing the remaining blade from its other arm, the metal goliath wielded both sword and flail, ready for the ghouls who dared to challenge the robust robot.

One of the lycanthropes that managed to survive the impact of the dead owl-man was the first to pounce its prey.

It was agile, yet its easily telegraphed attack was quickly detected by Ramona. The moment she glanced at its lunging arms, she lashed out with her reverse blade and made short work of its hands, each sliced off at the wrist. It tripped over its feet before standing up, unable to process this new tortuous sensation running through its body.

The wolf-man was too enraged to care. It then launched at the cerulean colossus with an open maw before a blade pierced its chest like so many of its allies. A second, more opportunistic, wolf creature slashed Draco Azul back. The impact of that swipe would have hurt, had the mech's new pilot not endured worse from her prior training session. Then the same lupine ghoul pounced once more at the blue guardian, but the mech slid its knife out of the foe in front and into the one behind it, puncturing the beast's left lung.

The pilot yelled out in fury as she dropped her weapons and grabbed onto each dying wolf's head. In one fell swoop, the two werewolf-like apparitions were smashed into each other in a collision that shattered their skulls. Blood splattered across the concrete of the adjacent houses, towers, and roads. Both ghouls slumped down on the ground, completely devoid of all life.

Ramona breathed heavily and was sweating profusely. The physical toll of controlling the mech during the encounter was taxing her body more than any battle she had previously fought. Even though thrill of the combat was intoxicating she now understood why it was hard at times for Eric to not lose himself in the middle of any given fight.

Ekchuah also took notice of how the fight was affecting her. He knew she was still recovering from the training she endured hours prior. If the AI's disciple continued to fight with this level of output, Ramona would soon suffer from burnout and rapidly succumb to the tremendous stress of Draco Azul's systems. If her state of mind were to be crushed by the raw power of the Primal Warrior, she'd be left wide open for the Nagual and his army to shred the mech into pieces.

"Don't waste your energy right away," Eckhuah warned his new pupil. "We still have to worry about their boss. These guys are just small fries."

Heeding the AI's words, Ramona breathed in then exhaled to compose herself as she picked up her blades. The young pilot readied herself with both sabers in hand, not foreseeing any ambushes from above. Yet another bat creature latched onto Draco Azul's shoulders and penetrated the tough armor. The cockpit sparked from the damage the mech took outside.

Ramona felt herself lifted from the floor as the system replicated the sensation of the metallic warrior rising against its pilot's will. Being a virtual hologram, Ekchuah remained stationary, unphased by the tremors. Utilizing all its power, the winged horror soared in the air with the others waiting to get their chance to swarm their enemy.

"Ekchuah!" Ramona called out to her AI companion. "Activate the wings for just a moment! I have an idea!"

"All you need to do is shout 'Draco Wings!'"

Ramona did just that and soon enough, the rocket powered wings emerged from Draco Azul's back and propelled the mech higher than the beast carrying the robot had intended. The bat-like monstrosity was forced to disengage its tight clutch. Once freed, the mech shifted directions and propelled both of its blades right into the ghoul's wings, severing them. As the wingless beast fell to the Earth below, several more airborne demons aimed their fangs and talons at the blue guardian.

Each wild fiend was met with an onslaught of vigorous slices and kicks. In an act of desperation, the largest of the bat-like creatures forced itself into a grapple hold with the giant robot and plummeted the two of them into the city below like a meteorite. When they collided to the ground, the vampire took the brunt of the impact, breaking every bone in its body and rupturing all its internal organs.

While heavily bruised, Ramona stood back up in a matter of seconds. Surrounding her on all sides were the last of the giant and semi-giant wolf-men.

"Tu te lo buscaste," the pilot confidently said as she readied the Draco Fangs, telling her opponents that they were asking for the pain she was happy to deliver.

Each hairy abomination came at her with a plethora of claws and teeth at their disposal. Yet, each swipe and every bite was countered with a flurry of jabs, slices, kicks, and elbows. Scratches and gashes now adorned the azure goliath, but no amount of pain could hurt Ramona more than the very thought of losing Eric, the person who gave her life a new purpose. He had saved her life before, and she was ready to return the favor. What she was experiencing was practically numb to her. Finally, one lone wolf-man attempted to get back up from a previous beating. Yet, the moment it was back on its feet a roped blade flew into its chest.

"¡Ven para acá!" shouted the rookie pilot as she pulled the man-wolf close enough to plunge her other sword into its body, finishing it off for good.

Without warning, an immense scream seemingly ceased all action on the battlefield as every ghoul in the vicinity refrained from fighting at that very moment. Inside the mech, Ramona covered her ears from the mind-numbing projection, which lasted for a minute. To the woman, it lasted an eternity.

"Ahh, what is this!" screamed Ramona as she covered her ears in a vain attempt to silence the echoing noise.

"It's hard to tell since it's not picking up on any of my radars," replied Ekchuah, who was shifting between various screens with zero results.

Ramona opened her eyes and through Draco Azul's telescopic vision, attempted to scan the entire area. Eventually, her enhanced view picked up a familiar pale figure atop the Cathedral of Chihuahua. Far enough away to avoid the carnage, the Nagual had been witnessing the massacre that befell his family. The master of the ghouls vigorously shook from head to toe, as if he was screaming. It must be a mental projection, Ramona theorized. She thought to strike the extraterrestrial, before the shrieking suddenly went silent.

The alien being then set its sights on the blue juggernaut. Ramona recognized that gaze from before, back when it shared its thoughts and emotions with her. Somehow, she could tell he was not looking at Draco Azul, but right at her.

"It didn't have to be this way!" Ramona called out through the exterior intercom.

Draco Azul pointed one of its blades at the Nagual.

Oh, but it did, the Nagual telepathically exclaimed while he jumped off the tall, devastated skyscraper.

His body increased in size, nails erupted out of its fingers, elongating and becoming sharp. The entity's tail bone extended out and morphed into a long, hairy appendage. The vampire's pale skin grew white fur with gray spots as his skull restructured to a more feline silhouette. The Nagual met face to face with Draco Azul, now in the form of a white jaguar with beaming emerald eyes. Among his countless transformations, the albino cat grew to become his favorite over the ages. Thanks to the infusion of the Diablo's blood, consumed in order to control his unhinged brood, the vampiric being's body was far stronger than it had ever been. Ramona's eyes widened at the realization that the Nagual had become a hybrid like his minions.

"Especially after everything I lost!" The Nagual snarled at the humongous robot through his newly formed mouth. "And you've only added to my pain and misery!"

The newly enlarged enemy leapt at Draco Azul before the robot had time to unleash its rope-wielded, dart-like weapon. When he reached his target, the giant feline reached out and grasped the mech's horned helmet with its extended talons.

144

The abhorrent monstrosity planted the machine's face into the ground, after which he hooked its legs within his arm as he forced one of his digitigrade feet on the Primal Warrior's back. The mastermind of the ghouls then proceeded to pull the robot's limbs into a painful leg lock.

Learning this maneuver from human entertainment, the Nagual had been motivated by the same Mexican professional wrestling Ramona took inspiration from. He believed some of those moves would come in handy if he ever had to fend for himself against a powerful opponent. Inside Draco Azul, the pilot's lower spine strained from the severe brutality. She shoved one of her blades into one of the vampire's calves. He roared in pain, the reaction allowing the azure knight to finally free itself from his hold. The mechanical giant stood tall once more.

Then the automaton placed both blades on its forearms as the felinoid vampire extended his claws and bared his fangs. The Nagual swiftly impaled his talons into the massive mech's chest cavity, piercing through Draco Azul's thick armor and narrowly missing its pilot. Sparks flew across the room as the mechanical appendages that would aid Ekchuah in defending the inner sanctum of the metal goliath were rendered inoperable.

"Aah!" Ramona shrieked in a combination of stinging pain and righteous fury as she felt like a steak knife had stabbed through her ribs.

"Don't wanna worry you, but we got a breach!" Ekchuah called out.

"Yeah," said the panting aviator, trying and failing to hide her torturous ordeal. "I can tell."

The Nagual opened his jaguar-like maw as it prepared to bite down on his rival's head before a massive fist entered his jaws instead. Ramona marched forward, each step bringing the vampire's claws inching ever so closer to where she stood.

"Ramona, watch it!" warned the panic-stricken AI. He forced one of the remaining internal cameras to of the cockpit to display in his pupil's visor. "His claws are moving towards you, and I can't get the security systems to work!"

"Don't worry," responded the novice. "I think I got this."

Draco Azul lifted its other arm and threw a punch right into the albino jaguar's stomach, forcing the beast-man to lose his grip on the robot's chassis. Finally freed from his grasp, Ramona seized the moment by propelling the shapeshifter into the chapel where the leader of the ghouls had once hid.

Once the young woman forced her opponent into the building, Ramona delivered one punch after another, never giving the blood-drenched feline a chance to get back up. As she ruthlessly assaulted the enemy, her muscles twinged as she felt an intense pain spreading throughout her body as she slowed down. The adrenaline that had kept her going this long had begun to wear off. Every affliction she had received in battle was coming at her in full force while her endurance was depleting.

Before Ramona could pass out, she stepped away from her foe and kneeled to catch her breath. Unfortunately for her, she had no time to rest. Several of the Nagual's human-sized followers surrounded their fallen messiah. Through the mechanical titan's eyes, the pilot deduced that these were the normal variety of pale humanoid ghouls. The vampire and the metallic warrior stood in a moment of silence. Both combatants' bodies were covered in scars and wounds, neither ceasing in their goal to overcome the other.

"We got company."

Ekchuah shifted Ramona's view to one of the external cameras. There, she witnessed another barrage of the owl and bat people covering Draco Azul's body, all aiming for the gashes the Nagual left on the robot's chest. Each of them sensed the human life that rested inside and yearned to consume her delicious plasma.

146

"¡Maldita sea!" Ramona irately shouted.

CHAPTER 14

In the void of pure darkness, Eric Martinez's eyelids slowly opened. He first saw a blinding white light, which faded into a dark blood red sky as he blinked, but he could not tell if it was daylight or nighttime. The pilot of Draco Azul got to his feet, noticed he had no shirt on, no footwear, and only a tattered pair of jeans. His upper body was as pale as the moon. The young pilot's transformation was worsening.

Eric was freezing from the cold air while he felt horrified by what he witnessed all around him. It was Chihuahua City, only completely desolate and utterly devoid of all life. The once beautiful architecture of the landscapes, skyscrapers, communities, and temples were reduced to smoldering ash and rubble. Eric paced through the surreal new world he found himself in with the echoes of burning objects, creatures howling from afar, and an ice cold breeze.

From a distance, two thin, filthy, scarred men fought over what looked like a half-eaten leg. The two screamed at each other like children arguing over their favorite toy in class. One of the feral men overpowered the other and bit into whatever meat was left on the marrow. In a matter of seconds, the other man sank his yellow teeth into his rival's thighs, continuing his meal on his acquaintance, who was too starved to notice as he gnawed on his prized bone.

Eric was appalled by how very inhuman these people acted. However, as the disturbing act of cannibalism unfolded, the young man could not help but notice the injuries both men had as they fed. They appeared as if they were branded with hot irons, a visual he could not help but recall from some place, though he was unable to quite pin down what it was. Passing by the two, Eric felt that he had more important matters to attend to, not to mention he was poorly equipped to handle such bizarre circumstances.

Venturing forth, Eric found more humans, though in a more passive state of mind, sitting by a fire blankly staring into the burning flames. They all looked as if none of them had any semblance of consciousness left in their minds. He called to them as he got closer, waved his hand in front of their faces, yet none responded. They all appeared withered and thin.

Were they intentionally starving themselves to death? Eric wondered. *Had they all given up on living?*

He left the strange tribe to pursue his investigation of this new environment. The pilot eventually came across the edge of a cliff, where he peered off into the distance. There, he was shocked to discover endless giant craters, deeper and wider than Meteor Crater in Arizona. Eric wondered if he had woken up to a world ravaged by multiple asteroids.

Continuing his stroll, the young man noticed a giant structure in the distance. It was too far to make out what it could be, but something compelled him to find out. As he approached the construction, he began to recognize details. Thoughts raced through his mind as he prayed to God it was not what he believed it to be. Finally, he realized the monstrous monument was indeed the battered remains of Draco Azul's head. Half buried in the dead soil, its eyes were shattered, its horn was broken in half, and its once bright blue and white armor had faded into a burnt shadow of its once glorious visage.

Eric moved around the detached cranium and was left speechless as the further remains of the Primal Warrior were also buried in the sand, a blade here and a foot there. Some had exposed rusted wires and armor. Judging from the damage, the young hero believed they were forcefully ripped apart. It was as if a Diablo, or something worse, was able to finally best the seemingly unbeatable machine.

As traumatizing a visual as this was, Eric was not convinced that any of it was real. Like the classroom from before, everything about this world had the Nagual's signature written all over it. This must be his twisted perception of an ideal world, one where his kind ruled all, leaving the scraps of humanity to fend for themselves. At this point, Eric was waiting for the blood sucker to reveal himself and monologue about how much better this world was.

"A travesty this world will come to," spoke the devil from up above.

Eric searched for the source of the voice and found his foe standing atop the mech's head. While he still had no mouth, the Nagual's voice sounded as if it was said out loud in this surreal land.

The alien jumped off the destroyed machine and gracefully landed in front of Eric.

"Yeah, your vision of the future is just lovely," the pilot sarcastically commented.

"Oh, this is not of my doing, child. This isn't what I want for the planet. Why don't you look at that broken home over there?"

The Nagual pointed at a half destroyed suburban house. Eric stepped carefully through the remains of the damaged household and peaked his head through the opening. What he saw haunted him. A little boy and his mother struggled to stay warm. Covering their barely clothed bodies were keloid scars and burns, marks that could only come from the aftermath of a nuclear explosion.

When Eric was a history teacher, one event he taught his students was the bombing of Hiroshima and Nagasaki in 1945. Even during his studies in college he had examined numerous archived photographs of the direct aftermath of the horrific bombings. He stepped back and tripped onto the ruins, aghast at the realization.

"Do you understand now?" spoke the Nagual, who suddenly stood before the shocked Eric. "This macrocosm of devastation is not the result of my influence, but by the plague that is man. Greed, power, and ignorance poisoned the world. War after war, bomb against bomb, genocide following genocide. These are the pitfalls that your race will drive themselves into. This is why my brood must replace them."

Eric slumped to the cracked foundation that was once luscious green grass. He always knew human beings were capable of self-destruction, as he had studied it for numerous years. However, there was no way they could end it all like this.

Could they?

"This is exactly what I want to avoid," the alien continued. "Your kind doesn't have true social bounds. Rather, your kind believes in self-scrutinization, judging anyone that differs from themselves or a collective unit they've attached themselves to. It's a truly depraved philosophy. Country, religion, race, gender, and all shapes and sizes. Each one, a category to divide yourselves among and weaponize against one another.

"Even amongst these social bubbles you're never safe as it's only a matter of time before you start stabbing each other in the back. Everyone's out for themselves, and no good deed occurs without an ulterior motive. That's why they must become one with the Nagual bloodline, where they'll finally live in a pure society where all are equal."

The Nagual stretched out a hand to Eric, enticing him to join his cause since he believed that he had finally gotten through to the silent listener.

"Join me by my side, and together we can usher in an era of tranquility. A brand new haven to call our own," the Nagual told Eric.

The confused warrior stared at the unworldly palm of the vampire as he thought about the Nagual's words. Eric

151

initially refused to believe he was right, but the more his enemy spoke, the more sense he started making. But were these his own thoughts, or had the ghoulish virus finally gotten a hold of his brain? Still, he could not ignore the factual evidence given the former teacher's knowledge about humanity's history. If the past and present were anything to go by, this possibility could very well become a reality. Would the Nagual's methods truly save humanity?

Eric slowly extended his hand, compelled to seal his deal with the devil as if he had no other option. Every scenario that flashed through his mind had always resulted in death and failure. Each dark thought drew his hand closer to the white palm of the being that promised salvation.

"Aah!"

Eric recognized that voice as Ramona's. Wherever it was coming from, he realized it had to be emanating from the outside world. The main pilot of Draco Azul suddenly remembered what was at stake. It was not just humanity who was close to losing everything, but so was his friend who had volunteered to put her life on the line. He continued to hear her cries, like she was experiencing a level of pain unlike any other. The woman's intense struggle were more than the pilot could bear. His mind flashed back to the Rodriguez family, the very people he failed to protect in Ensenada. That day he promised himself that never again would he allow any harm to come to the innocents.

Yet, until now, he had done nothing but let himself be consumed by fear and pessimism, whether it was from his own inner demons or the Nagual's virus. Meanwhile, his friends were left to suffer on the battlefield. Eric knew he would slowly become a monster, but he would be damned if he was going to allow the Nagual to hurt Ramona anymore. Neither her, nor anyone else would suffer as long as he had anything to say about it.

For a brief moment he pondered if protecting humanity would be a fruitless cause. As long as he still had life in him, he would do his best in setting the path for mankind to prosper, alongside Ramona and Ekchuah. Eric's veins pulsed, his heart rate increased, and his eyes glowed an incandescent green. It was at this point that the Nagual realized the futility of his actions.

"Here's what I think of your haven!"

Eric punched the vampire right in the face while roaring in anger. Like when he first awakened in the imagined post-apocalyptic landscape, the world around the two became illuminated. At last, Eric's eyes snapped open again to the familiar metal walls of his resting quarters. Outside the room, the bed-ridden Eric heard Ekchuah activating the security system along with the sounds of metal ripping apart, indicating the enemy had once again bypassed the outer layers of Draco Azul's armor. He quickly stood up and began feeling an intense sensation unlike anything he had experienced before.

Looking at his hands once more, Eric realized he had grown completely pale. His nails had grown into claws, his muscles burned as he felt a strange combination of heat and hunger. Having biologically become a ghoul himself, his metabolism was burning energy at a rapid rate, requiring him to feast in order to keep his strength up. It must be the very same thing that drove the mindless slaves of the Nagual to turn rabid.

However, he would not let his hunger control him as long as he was still conscious. He looked down at a brown leather coat that had provided warmth during his recovery. It was the very same coat the head of the Rodriguez household gave him months ago. His memories of the family, along with his bonds with his friends, were what ultimately saved him from the brink of insanity. He wore the coat over his bare back as a constant reminder of his humanity, before using all of his newfound power to bring down the locked metallic door.

* * *

Eric stood before his friends and the intruders. Ekchuah and Ramona were unsure what was going to happen next as their comrade now appeared nearly unrecognizable with his ghostly skin and glowing eyes. His friends wondered if he would attempt to attack Ramona. The former pilot instead ran towards the revenants. Using his superhuman strength, the man grabbed the first beast before tearing his victim apart limb by limb with ease. He shifted focus to the other invaders, who now kept their focus solely on him.

They lunged at him, the seemingly defenseless Eric disappearing beneath a flurry of teeth and claws. However, within seconds he overpowered the entire pack, lifting them off his person and systematically executing each savage challenger. He began hyperventilating after the brutal display of raw power.

"E-Eric?" Ramona sputtered out, needing to know if her friend was still there. Ramona and the AI were appalled by the violence Eric inflicted on the malicious creatures trespassing in the cockpit. However, Eric raised up his right arm and gave her and Ekchuah the sign they needed, a victorious thumbs up and warm smile.

"Dang, kid, we thought we lost you there for a sec. How are ya feelin'?" Ekchuah asked his dearly missed partner. While he was glad Eric was in control of himself, there was no telling how long it would last.

"Like crap. But I'm still me. All thanks to you, Ramona." The woman was stunned by his words.

"Me? What did I do?"

"By reminding me what we're fighting for. Otherwise, I might've given in to the madness. I don't know how long I can keep this up, but I'll help out any way I can until then."

Tears flowed from Ramona's eyes upon hearing her companion's words.

"Alright, kid," the hologram responded. "You can start by keeping those ghouls at bay. Make sure they don't get to Ramona."

"Got it!"

Ekchuah then addressed his latest pupil. "Ramona, I hate to ask this, but can you still fight?"

"N-no problem! I can handle it," Ramona insisted, despite her wounds.

Eric chuckled a bit, recalling when they last trained together. The moment of elation ended, and it was time to get back to business. Meanwhile, the AI was still unsure of his team's current state. He did not want to risk the lady's life again, not after all she had to suffer. Unfortunately, he also knew Eric was in no condition to carry the torch. Whether he liked it or not, Ramona would have to be the one to put an end to the dark reign of the Nagual and his horrid followers.

"Alright. Me and the kid can deal with those blood suckers while you take out the head honcho."

Ramona smiled as her mentor trusted her to finish the task at hand.

"Thanks, coach. Hey, Eric!"

The young woman quickly pulled him into a great big hug. Eric, afraid of what his new strength may do to her, placed a trembling hand over her back. Both siblings-in-arms began to relax as they simultaneously placed their faith in one another. Neither of them knew what was about to ensue, yet they took comfort in knowing that whatever happens, they would face it together.

"Stay with us," said Ramona.

"And you keep up the fight," Eric responded.

Ramona returned to the central panel and placed the visor over her head, controlling Draco Azul once more. Eric and Ekchuah positioned themselves by the opening in the cockpit should more of the Nagual's brood try to make another unexpected visit. The blue colossus rose back up, its body sparking from all the damage it endured. Each shock sent a jolt of pain through Ramona's still recovering body. She did her best to work through the agony and focus on locating the target. Dust and fragments of the fallen structures fell off the mighty machine.

The jaguar-like creature witnessed his foe's resurrection from afar, dumbfounded as to how it was still capable of standing. His followers hissed, shrieked, and growled at the mech with a burning desire to tear it apart.

Was it the boy? he thought. *Was* he *behind this?*

Not only did Eric escape his mental grasp, but had he managed to best his family? The Nagual again attempted to pry into the minds within the azure knight. Yet, something was blocking him. As much as he tried, the only thing he could sense was an intense bond, one fueled by love, trust, and courage. It was the very thing he yearned for yet had failed to replicate with his pseudo-family.

A harrowing thought then entered the Nagual's mind as he considered if perhaps he had been wrong. The ghoul began to wonder if humanity was truly capable of something so pure. No, he thought. They only sought to mock him and his efforts. He would prove his cause was the righteous one. He beckoned to the last of his clan in preparation for the conclusion to their showdown.

"How much power do we have left, coach?" asked the backup pilot.

"Only enough to last half an hour."

Ramona nodded and faced the monitor, staring right into the eyes of the undeterred leader of the undead army.

"That's more than enough," said Ramona as she cracked her knuckles and repositioned her weapons.

156

In one hand, the bladed scarf. In the other, the Draco Fang. The Nagual growled in anger. Regardless of their bond and mental fortitude, they were still too weak-minded to see the bigger picture. To him, these humans were willing to put everything into protecting their doomed race.

"It's too late, foolish humans!" the albino beast bellowed. "I've come too far to have it all end here. Not after all I've been through. If you wish to die by your own negligence, then allow us to send you all to the burning depths of Hell!"

The Nagual and his followers stampeded towards the Primal Warrior. No allies were around to assist in taking out the sheer number of abominations. Despite the immense odds, Team Draco stood their ground. Ramona began her assault against the first wave of the Nagual's accursed creations, swinging her scarf blade in circular patterns to slice up any approaching creature. The few that managed to bypass her defense were stabbed with a giant blade to the head, torso, or stomach without a moment's hesitation from the reinvigorated pilot.

One of the wolf-men sunk its razor sharp teeth into the goliath's forearm, which was a grave miscalculation. Draco Azul repeatedly punched the canine's nostrils until it released its hold as the beast bled profusely. Then, the battle-hardened machine swung its Draco Fang to puncture the attacker's beating heart. The giant robot kept pushing forward, forcing its saber to skewer more of the werewolf's ghoulish brethren into becoming a gruesome shish kabob.

As Ramona laid waste to the savage leviathans, several more of the smaller owl, bat, and wolf-men crawled their way up the mechanical warrior's massive frame in a second attempt to destroy the weapon from within. However, as they passed through the rips and tears their fallen comrades made for them previously, they were met with the duo of one Eric Martinez and his holographic cohort. Together, the pair slayed each beast that breached the hull of their humanoid vessel, Eric going for their throats as Ekchuah fried them with his tasers.

"Amazing," Ekchuah commented, watching his student snap a head-locked wolf-man's neck. "I've never seen any of these guys carry half the strength you've got!"

"I know," said the exhausted man as he held back the claws of another bat creature. "I think it has something to do with how quickly they burn away their energy. Heads up!"

Eric threw the winged rodent into Ekchuah's range, allowing the AI to electrocute it until all its skin was singed to a crisp.

"My theory," Eric continued, "is that they waste most of their energy in pursuit of nourishment. Because of their wild nature, these things are in a constant state of frenzy."

"I see. So, as long as you're in control, you can conserve your strength until it's needed."

"Pretty much," said a shrugging Eric.

"Works for me!" grinned the hologram.

Outside the mech, three more brutes were sliced open by the Draco Víbora, which was now stuck in a nearby building. Ramona sighed in frustration, having made the mistake twice now. She commanded the robot to pull the scarf back while backing away from the ghouls it had just slaughtered.

"Ah!" screamed the pilot as she grabbed onto her shoulder.

"What's wrong?" asked Eric.

"D-don't worry about me. Must've done something to my shoulder."

Ramona loosened the scarf from her weapon and held both blades in hand. She realized that swinging Draco Víbora around had done considerable damage to her joints and thus needed to retire the strategy for the time being.

"I can help with that," suggested Ekchuah. "I got a device that'll-"

"Sorry, but we can't waste any more time," Ramona interrupted as she peered down to see several more human-sized ghouls crawling up the mech. "You guys still have work to do."

While her male companions tended to their guests, the woman rubbed each of the massive knives against one another as a warning to any hellspawn that dared to step up to the plate. Taking the bait, the next wave of erratic creatures proceeded, having no care for the consequences. All that was on their one-track mind was to destroy and feast upon the lifeforce they sensed deep within the machine.

From a distance, the Primal Warrior found its real target, the Nagual. He was resting, trying to recuperate and regain his impressive strength. Ramona needed to bypass all the drones to get at their leader and she knew exactly how to do it.

Draco Azul sprinted to the stampede of revenants. Right before it connected with the next wave, the colossal robot jumped up in the air and impaled its blades on one of the harpy-like abominations, shifting its body into aiming towards its leader. From below, the lycanthropes reached out to the metal guardian, only to receive a fury of stomps to their faces. Draco Azul seesawed its body before flinging itself right towards the source of the chaos. Ramona slammed her fist point blank into the Nagual's face, cracking its skull with a powerful wallop. She proceeded to elbow Nagual in the gut, knee him in the chest, and advanced with continuous slashes to the chest with both Draco Fangs held in her trademark reverse-grip fashion.

As Eric and Ekchuah fought off another wave of the demonic undead, the sapphire automaton affixed its left blade back on its forearm. Ramona then used her less injured arm to wrap the villain's chest with her scarf. Mustering all the raw willpower Ramona had left to give, she had the metal goliath swing her enemy around and slammed the jaguar to the pavement numerous times. Any ghoul that tried to intervene felt the wrath of the exhausted pilot as she bashed every one of them with their creator.

"Draco Wings!" Ramona called with confidence.

Draco Azul unfolded its impressive wingspan. It launched into the sky and took its monstrous adversary along for the ride. The Primal Warrior threw the entangled Nagual further into the air and unwrapped it before rocketing towards the nefarious killer.

"¡Toma!" she yelled in righteous anger as she impaled him in the chest with the lone blade she held in her hands.

She then held the feline abomination with her weapon and flew back down to Earth at a rapid pace. Within the mech, the pilot felt nauseous, doing everything she could to keep herself from vomiting. Yet, she kept going in the hopes she would finally put an end to this madness.

Draco Azul tossed its opponent into the ground, releasing the Draco Fangs from his body. Beside her, Eric held on for dear life to one of the wall's mechanical arms to avoid flying out of the torn holes around them. Ramona lifted the mech back up before descending to the ground at a slower speed. She took in as much air as she could, feeling as though the battle had finally come to a long awaited conclusion.

The blood sucker twirled uncontrollably as he fell from the heavens. After a brief descent below, the cat-man crashed into the outskirts of the city as Draco Azul landed nearby, attaching its last blade to its arm.

To everyone's shock, the Nagual was still very much alive. His body bruised and broken, he wobbled towards his rival before his legs finally gave out. The azure knight now loomed over the decrepit form that was the Nagual. His body had numerous cuts and puncture wounds, too many to be able to survive for long. Defeated, the vampire knew this, at last realizing the futility of his actions.

No words could express the amount of rage he felt towards the injustice he had suffered. Numerous centuries of surviving, hiding, planning, and murdering had borne no fruit for the immortal being, but only further pain and misery.

The distressing creature howled at the heavens. Ramona could hear the ground rumbling as the last remnants of the ghouls were following the call of their master.

"No way!" Ramona cried out.

"Can't this guy take the hint?" said Ekchuah. "He's lost."

Eric followed up. "Guess he wants to drag this out to the bitter end."

Ramona attempted to silence the vampire. However, it did not take long for his family to arrive. The bat and owl-men landed themselves between the Nagual and Draco Azul. The wolf-men followed suit. However, they were not paying attention to the giant robot they had been fighting all this time, nor were his flying minions. They were all gazing upon the Nagual who, despite his injuries, stood tall in a futile effort to intimidate his foe.

"This is far from over. We would rather die than surrender to you monsters," growled the battered creature. "My family and I will battle till our dying breath. Now, my brethren, attack!"

None of the beasts made a move.

"What are you waiting for? The enemy is there!"

The Nagual used as much of his mental abilities as he could, yet not a single creature followed his commands. Rather, they all began leering at the bloodied form of their supposed leader. In a sudden act of treachery, one of the Nagual's followers bit his master's arm. As the alien struggled to pry off the beast, another followed the first one's lead and clamped down on his shoulder before a third minion went for his leg. The Nagual fought them off but was soon overpowered in a frenzy as every ghoul bit into the flesh of the distraught vampire.

"What are you doing?" he cried. "Stop! We're family!"

What the lead ghoul always feared had now come to pass. Ever since he used the Diablo's blood to strengthen his army, his control over them weakened, if only slightly. Now, the Nagual's strength was a sliver of what it once was, meaning he could no longer control the actions of his ghouls. The moment they smelled his fresh wounds, their unhinged bloodthirsty nature took over as their degraded minds no longer saw him as their ally, but as nourishment.

Team Draco were in shock at what was transpiring before them. All members fell silent, unable to come to grips with the horrible fate that had befallen the Nagual. The alien continued to attempt to reason with his brood, as he was unwilling to lay a finger on the unit he had deluded himself into thinking were his kin. Instead, the ravenous fiends continued to sink their teeth into his body and tore his skin and muscles to shreds. They clawed their way to his bones and organs, consuming anything to calm their insatiable hunger.

He pleaded to them again, and all he could see were the soulless unfeeling eyes of the monsters he created. He knew they were savage but had hoped that he would show these lost souls the means of becoming true Naguals; that they would become a real family someday.

Looking at the sixty-meter behemoths that preyed upon his flesh and shed his blood, he wondered if there was ever any chance at raising such violent creatures. Was the familial bond he desperately craved for an impossibility? He set his sights on Draco Azul. Radiating from the blue titan was indeed a true bond. A beautiful, precious one that deserved to prosper.

"Ramona!" the dying Nagual cried out. "You need to end this now!"

The young woman was taken aback.

"What? B-but you'll die!"

"I'd rather suffer an eternity in Hell than an eternity in isolation!"

Ramona understood the creature's dying wish and positioned herself to unleash the one attack she promised never to use. It was Draco Azul's most devastating blow, the Draco Striker.

"Wait, Ramona!" protested Ekchuah. "We don't know if you'll survive this!"

"What? Is this true?" Eric responded.

Ramona ignored the pair as she charged up the attack. "Draco...!"

Before she could unleash the large amounts of lightning stored in the robot's central horn, the trainee pilot noticed tears streaming from the Nagual's eyes. She knew he deserved retribution for the actions he committed for his warped desires, yet still she wept for the tragic creature.

"J-just... finish it!" the Nagual called out to Ramona in his dying breath, overcome by sheer agony as his army began to tear off his limbs and rip out his organs.

At that point, nothing else could be done for the doomed creature. Ramona finished accumulating enough energy for the final blow. She could feel an enormous weight on her head and her body rattling as Draco Azul's horn pulsed with electricity and the immense amount of power grew and grew. It was time. The young woman concentrated and uttered the second of the two words required to draw the final curtain to a close.

"Striker!"

The Primal Warrior's horn erupted, releasing an immense, widening beam that became a colossal column of surging light heading towards the monsters. In his final moment, the Nagual saw the blinding flash of light approaching. He closed his eyes as the intense heat enveloped him and every one of the malicious beasts tearing at his lacerated form. After a booming explosion only a smoldering landscape remained of the extraterrestrial and his minions.

At that moment, the surviving members of the covenant roared out in pain all throughout Chihuahua City. None of them were able to comprehend the death of their leader. The lot of them slumped to the ground, as each of their bodies morphed back to who they were before their leader tainted them. In the cockpit, Ramona wheezed from the amount of stress that the last attack had put on her body, and she was already struggling to stay conscious.

"Agh!" Eric shouted.

His connection to the Nagual had finally been severed and his body was finally reverting back to normal. The young man looked down at his hands. Color was returning as his own blood circulated through his veins.

"Alright!" exclaimed Eric, human once again.

"You guys did it!" said Ekchuah, elated that the battle was finally over, and that his first protégé was now free from the unbearable curse.

"Nice work, dear!" Ekchuah shouted to Ramona.

The young woman did her best to smile. Her whole body was shaking uncontrollably. At last, she succumbed to her injuries and fainted. She could not even feel how much it hurt when her body collided with the solid floor.

"Ramona? Ramona!"

Those were the last words she heard before closing her eyes.

CHAPTER 15

A city in ruins, murderous monsters, a creature seeking revenge, and a friend in danger. These images drifted through Ramona's unconscious mind. Such terrifying imagery repeated like a nightmarish playlist of the woman's most horrific memories. Her mind recalled the moment she and Eric were confronted by the massive bat creature that slaughtered the policemen and journalists. She thought back to when she first gazed upon the resentful eyes of the Nagual in Ojuela. Then she recollected the moment her beloved friend was assaulted by the fiendish Dogman who would infect him with a life-threatening disease.

The young woman felt alone and feared the thought of losing her closest friends. Suddenly, she remembered she was the only one capable of saving everyone, saving Eric. Her subconsciousness raced through the last 24 hours of her life, training in a simulation and facing off against foes from the past before she fended off wave after wave of atrocious beasts. She then recalled the moment everything ended in a piercing white light.

Ramona was not sure if it was all over. Her instincts were telling her that the living nightmare the city had been experiencing had not yet reached its conclusion. The struggle was never over. She had to carry on fighting for Eric, for Chihuahua City, for Mexico, for the entire planet.

The girl's eyes snapped open, and she gasped. She lifted her body over what appeared to be a medical bed, the same one she placed her companion in. Her eyes darted all around, but it did not take long to see Eric asleep, his back leaning against the wall right next to her. He did not seem to be infected by the Nagual's virus as his skin tone had returned to its original tanned appearance. The man was back to his normal self.

Exhilarated, Ramona rolled out of bed, only to find her legs barely capable of supporting her own weight, she was still weak from the battle. She shrieked when she landed on her resting companion's lap with a thud.

Eric snapped to attention before he noticed the bandaged woman laying on him. "Gah! What's happening? Are we under attack?"

"Ramona!" said the flustered man once he recognized the person on his lap. "What are you doing? Are you alright?"

The young woman laughed hysterically before bringing her friend in for a hug, overjoyed to finally speak to her dear loved one again. Eric chuckled as he too partook in the embrace.

"I'm fine, silly. It's you I was worried about."

"Heh. Yeah, I'm fine. All thanks to you."

Ramona removed herself from Eric's arms, only to notice the heavy bags under his eyes. Had it not been for his complexion, she would have thought he was still a ghoul.

"You look like you haven't slept in days."

Before the sleep-deprived man could speak, Ekchuah's hologram materialized in their room.

"That's because he hasn't. The kid's been watching over you the last two days as you recovered."

"Wait, I was out for that long?" asked a surprised Ramona. "What happened to the Nagual and all his ghouls?"

"The Nagual's gone forever," answered her male counterpart.

"Yup. You did good, dear. Damn good. Couldn't be prouder." The AI gave a hearty laugh. "Tell ya what. If you can do this well on your first try, maybe you should be our main pilot and Eric can be the backup."

Ramona giggled as Eric rolled his eyes.

"You were waiting to say that, weren't you?"

Ekchuah chuckled. "Heh. I'm just pulling your leg, kid. Like I told you earlier, you did a helluva job fighting through that virus and coming though. Both of you, actually. Despite everything, you guys buckled down when the going got tough and watched each other's backs in our darkest hour. I couldn't be prouder of the two of you."

Ramona and Eric both smiled, humbly, neither of them used to hearing such high praise from their teacher.

"If you don't mind," replied Ramona, "I think I'm gonna need a long break from piloting."

"It ain't as easy as it looks, huh?" said Eric as he flashed a grin.

"Hey, this doesn't mean I won't still kick your butt in sparring! My ribs may be broken, but I can go right now!"

The entirety of Team Draco roared in laughter. Ramona could finally relax as she and her friends reveled in their victory. Once her heart began to slow down, more questions were raised as to the fate of the city and everyone in it.

"So, what about the people of Chihuahua? Both the survivors and the infected. Last I remember, there are still plenty of ghouls left."

"Funny thing about that," the hologram said. "Once you took out their leader, every person he infected reverted to their original selves." Ekchuah hooked his thumb at his original pupil. "That's why Eric here is with us today and how he got us out of the city after you passed out."

"Guilty as charged," Eric sarcastically joked.

The AI opened a series of holographic screens, each highlighting different news outlets that were all reporting what had taken place in the aftermath of their battle. Hundreds of suddenly cured residents were under inspection by various physicians and psychologists. Those that had evacuated or had gone into hiding were desperately attempting to get in contact with any of their missing loved ones, be they dead or cured. The army had placed a quarantine in the center of the battlefield, fifty times larger than the previous one around the dead Diablo, in order to house every individual in the city for the time being.

Back in Mexico City, the government was already underway with plans to rebuild the city through the same funding process that allowed them to respond to previous, and most likely future, Diablo attacks.

"It's gonna be quite some time before those folks can have a normal life," uttered the humanoid hologram.

Eric responded. "I'll say. It was horrible killing someone who used to be human. Imagine how they must've felt when they were told they murdered God knows how many people."

"The worst thing is that none of it was their fault," said Ramona.

"Right," Ekchuah concurred. "Luckily, the government is giving the survivors a chance to reintegrate back into society, along with the uninfected once they've been processed."

"Thank God for that," frowned the young man. "Still, some scars will never heal, both physical and mental."

Ramona thought about Eric's words. Having lost her father at a young age through terrible circumstances, she sympathized with the people whose lives were forever changed, and those forever lost.

"There's just one thing I don't understand. How was it that everyone returned to normal when I killed the Nagual?"

Fortunately for her, Ekchuah, who had studied the bodies of various slain ghouls along with the Nagual's spilled blood during her two-day coma, had the answers.

"Well, it appeared I was right when I theorized that their survival rested on the Nagual's capabilities. You see, his species had this innate ability to both physically and mentally contort a victim's blood and body composition, essentially infecting them in order to act as their mindless servant. A powerful method of survival, I gotta say. It's a lot like those fungi that takes over the bodies of insects and gets them to spread their spores to other areas. Only, instead of reproduction, the Naguals must've originally utilized this ability for self-defense."

"But this one wanted to use his army for something else," commented Ramona. "He kept referring to them as his 'family.'" Then, it hit her. "I think he was trying to use his ability to make more Naguals."

Her eyes lowered to the ground upon realizing her fallen enemy's sad, delusional plan.

"I doubt that would've worked," added Eric. "Being a ghoul strips you of all reasoning. The only one in control would have to be that bastard. Trust me. I've been there and it ain't pretty."

Ekchuah proceeded with regaling his teammates with more of his analysis of the Nagual's biology.

"Still, it must've taken an enormous amount of mental strength to keep control of that many ghouls, especially over a ridiculously wide range between multiple cities. He had been around for centuries, though, so it's possible his abilities strengthened as he aged."

"Could explain why he waited until now to take over the world," suggested Eric.

His mentor agreed. "Right. Anyways, to make a long story short, once he was out of the picture his control over their biology ceased and everybody, dead and alive, reverted to their original form.

"The hybrid ghouls, on the other hand, weren't so lucky. Their unstable Diablo-ridden DNA did far more damage to them than anything the Nagual had done. Those that were still around rapidly decomposed into puddles of sludge. Let it be said that Nagual and Diablo blood combined is a recipe for disaster."

With her queries answered Ramona stared at a particular screen displaying a mass funeral for every one of the Nagual's victims from the last several days. Hundreds gathered around the perimeters of the quarantined area with candles and photographs of their deceased friends and family.

"That funeral has been going on ever since we left," Eric explained solemnly. "As if there weren't enough death already with the constant Diablo attacks."

A warm hand was placed over the tired man's shoulder.

"How about we join them?" Ramona suggested. "It'll provide us some closure."

A soft smile grew on Eric's face. "I like the sound of that. Hey, coach-"

"Say no more. I can handle it from here. Meanwhile, you two meanwhile get some rest. And for Christ's sake, Eric, sleep in the bed I made for you."

The hologram disappeared as he gestured to a second bed across the room of their resting quarters. It too folded out from the wall, only its blankets remained untouched.

"Heh sure thing," chuckled Eric.

"Where are we anyways?" asked the young woman.

"Off the coast of Cancun, almost submerged in the ocean. Ekchuah detected a lightning storm, and we stopped here for refueling since our energy was low."

As Eric helped Ramona get back in her bed, she still kept watch of the holographic screen showing the funeral.

"I wonder," she pondered, "if people treated the Nagual like these people do for those who passed away, maybe things would've been different."

It pained the lady to realize how humanity could be so cruel, unwilling to help a single lost soul. Especially an entire clan of refugees who only wanted to find a new home. She thought back to her early years growing up with Los Gigantes. Back then she had seen all kinds of cruelty but had never understood what drove people to do the things that they did.

Eric thought about his friend's words for a minute as he too watched the news broadcast. "Mankind can get really ugly at times. While I was fighting off the Nagual's control, he showed me a future where we all killed ourselves in a nuclear war. Given what our civilization has been through, I wouldn't say it was outside the realm of possibility. It was awful, simply awful."

"Eric, I'm so sorry."

"It's alright. Because as cruel as we have been, we're also capable of so much more."

Eric put his own hand on her shoulder.

"You showed me that. I hate to say it, but back there…" Eric paused as Ramona sensed his hand shaking. "I almost gave in to the Nagual. Even now I still don't know if it was me who wanted to give up on mankind or if it was him."

Ramona comforted her companion as she overlapped her hand over Eric's. Once more, her warmth provided comfort for the young man and his trembling stopped.

"But regardless, the moment I heard your voice… that's when I knew he was wrong, that there was beauty in humanity that's worth saving."

"One day, humanity will be more compassionate," she said.

Eric smiled. "By then, we'd be able to reach out to those in need before it's too late."

***

It was the third night since the Battle of Chihuahua. A massive, chained fence separated two camps of people. On one side were the former members of the Nagual's artificial clan, all adorned in clothing provided by their government and donated by the generous public.

Beside them were the number of survivors who had endured the vampire's wrath without ever knowing the circumstances behind their torture. Some had forgiven the actions of their once mind-controlled neighbors, while others did not feel ready to trust the people who had feasted on their loved ones.

Yet, both camps huddled together near the barrier of their encampment. Outside the fence was a growing number of people who had traveled to honor the dead and the scarred, each of whom held a candle, a cross, or a rosary. Men, women, and children alike had come to support the people of Chihuahua in their hour of need. Many brought food and clothing, whereas one pair brought enough canned food to feed ten families as they pushed a massive flatbed platform trolley. One of the latter two was a woman dressed in a leather jacket, while the other was a man in a large duster.

Several of the survivors thanked and blessed them for their donations, as too did the soldiers who accepted the platform trolley. The man and woman noticed a makeshift monument, hastily built as a memorial for the victims of the invasion. Similar monuments had been built before at the locations where the gigantic Diablos had appeared. Yet this one was far more intimate, as mankind had not yet experienced such a horrendous act of war. It was the shape of a massive wall decorated with hundreds of photos, each one a deceased cousin, a departed friend, a lost lover, a fallen sibling, a slain parent, a killed partner, or a perished family.

The man and woman walked up to the wall and carefully examined every single face that adorned the wall. Next to them, a woman placed a photo of a family, a mother, father, and little girl seemingly no older than ten.

"Are they family of yours?" asked the woman in her native tongue.

"Yes," replied the woman. *"My sister's, actually. I live down south. I came up here once I found out what happened. I tried getting in contact with them, but no one answered. Then I was told that they found their…"* she began to choke up before she could finish sharing.

"It's alright," the leather clad woman said. *"You don't need to tell us anymore."*

"I'm sorry," the crying woman apologized. *"I don't even know what to do now."*

The man in the long coat stepped forward. "We're truly sorry for your loss." He began to tear up. "Is there something we could do to help?"

The sorrowful woman was taken aback by his choice of language. He did not speak Spanish, but rather perfect English.

"Forgive my friend," said his female companion. *"He is from America. He can understand Spanish but has trouble speaking it. He's deeply sorry and asked if there's anything we can do to help."*

"That's perfectly fine. Well, if you can join me in prayer, I would appreciate that. I'm Ana, by the way."

"Our pleasure, I'm Ramona," said the woman.

"Eric," replied the man.

With the gathering of supporters, the three individuals stood together as they mourned the dead, lamented the tragedies that transpired, and hoped for a brighter tomorrow.

END

BONUS ART

All illustrations in this section are courtesy of artist Grace Henshaw.

Nagual (True Form)

Nagual (Shadow)

Nagual (Beast Form)

ABOUT THE AUTHORS

Andres Perez is a freelance editor and creator of the indie comic *Primal Warrior Draco Azul*. He spent six years living in Japan working as a conversational English teacher where he developed his skills as a writer. Andres is also a published author himself, having written the short story anthology *Draco Azul: Full Metal Chronicles*, published by Wild Hunt Press; co-written with Matthew Dennion the post-apocalyptic kaiju/mecha crossover novel *Atomic Rex: Ballad of Bravura*, published by Severed Press; and the self-published offbeat crossover comic book *Draco Azul/Atomic Rex: Shadow of the Raptor*.

As an editor, Andres has worked on projects such as the giant monster comic *Nagoraiar: Against the Terror of the Moon* by Garayann; the mythology-themed urban fantasy novel series *Gods' Wrath: Tournament of the Divine* and the dark comedy web comic *The Crookedman and his not so scary Crooked Catgirl*, both by William Kearney and published by Crookedlore Productions. He is also an online content creator who makes reviews and podcasts covering movies, television, comics, and games on his YouTube channel KaijuNoir.

Ace Marrok is an aspiring filmmaker and author. He was born in Staten Island, New York with a passion for creative writing. His stories delve into deep gray morals, with no simple right or wrong. Ace is also a freelance artist with styles ranging from cartoons, manga, and paintings.

Ace's debut publication is the novella *League of Heroes: Crucified*, which is a collaboration with sci-fi thriller novelist Matthew Dennion (*Atomic Rex; Chimera: Scourge of the Gods; Agent 666; Raptor: Retribution of the Revenants*; and many more), courtesy of Antithes Publishing,

181

Mexico is under siege by nightmarish beasts! Fortunately, an ancient mech has risen to the occasion, with a rookie pilot and his A.I. coach at the helm. Now, this metal goliath must stand against these demons before all hope is lost. Enter: DRACO AZUL! *Primal Warrior Draco Azul* is a 3-issue comic book series written by Andres Perez and illustrated by Tyler Sowles! Now <u>on sale at Amazon!</u>

Chaos has ravaged Mexico ever since nightmarish monsters mysteriously began erupting periodically from beneath the Earth's crust. In that time, hope came in the form of an ancient mechanical giant that had laid dormant since the days of the Maya civilization. Its name: Draco Azul!

Wielding this centuries-old extraterrestrial mech and guided by an A.I. mentor, civilian-turned-rookie pilot Eric Martinez must face these immeasurable threats, or else humanity is doomed. These are the tales of Eric's trials and tribulations as he faces off against extradimensional invaders, alien monstrosities, virtually simulated terrors, and more! All while learning the secrets of Draco Azul's past, present, and potential future.

Meanwhile, in another time and place, lies a world desolated by war. Within what was once the United States of America, humankind fights a desperate struggle against the gargantuan mutants that roam the land, as well as each other. For one former soldier, the continuation of civilization is of no importance to him. Armed with his towering war machine, he has only one thing on his mind: Survival.

Draco Azul: Full Metal Chronicles is a single author anthology by Andres Perez and published by Wild Hunt Press now available on Amazon!

DRACO AZUL & ATOMIC REX
SHADOW of the RAPTOR

A deadly illness is being spread through the city affecting the robot population. Reports indicate that a strange being is the source of the illness. With the police uninterested in solving crimes involving mechs, the case falls to two hard-nosed private eyes: Draco Azul and Atomic Rex. One of them is a By- the- numbers mech and the other is a short-tempered kaiju with a heart of gold. These two PI's will travel through a world of mechs and monsters besieged by a horror beyond imagination as they chase attempt to stop an enemy that is beyond their ability to comprehend.

Draco Azul/Atomic Rex: Shadow of the Raptor is a crossover collaboration in comic book form by authors Andres Perez and Matthew Dennion, bringing together their respective characters from kaiju fiction into an offbeat crime noir spoof! And you can get it on Amazon right this very second!

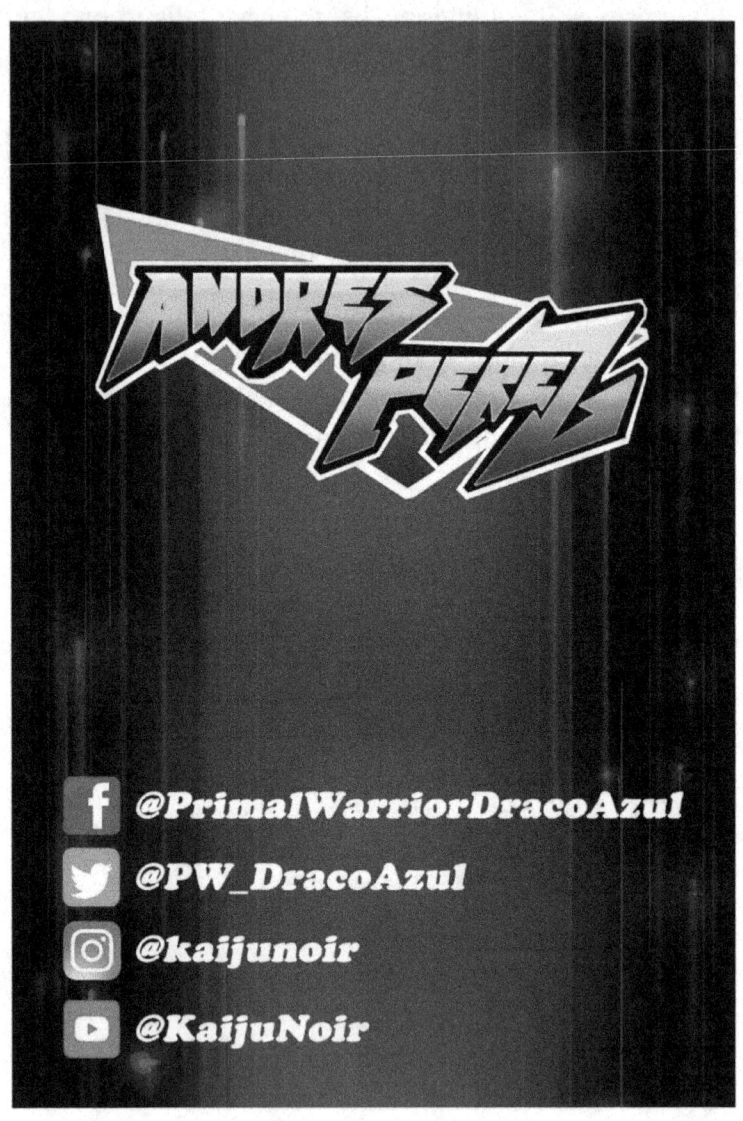

f @PrimalWarriorDracoAzul

🐦 @PW_DracoAzul

📷 @kaijunoir

▶ @KaijuNoir

A war is about to be waged, forcing heroes and monsters to work together against a galactic force beyond their imagination. Some factions will side with the heroic forces, and others will oppose. Heroes such as Talos, Raptor and the kaiju known as Gargantasaurus are in the forefront and now face a defiant and bitter kaiju, Arakana, for being betrayed by humanity whom it once protected. Can they make Arakana see the light or will its hatred lead to dire consequences?

League of Heroes: Crucified is Ace Marrok's debut novella, where he brings together super-heroes and kaiju created by editor (and author) Matthew Dennion as they are forced to band together against a galactic level foe that threatens the entire Earth. You can get it on Amazon now!

www.ingramcontent.com/pod-product-compliance
Lightning Source LLC
Chambersburg PA
CBHW060813120626
46557CB00001B/199